HARD HEARTS

MIKE MCCRARY

BAD
WORDS INC.

CONTENTS

Have a heart that never hardens, and a temper that never tires, and a touch that never hurts.
- Charles Dickens

The Edge... there is no honest way to explain it because the only people who really know where it is are the ones who have gone over.
- Hunter S. Thompson

PART ONE

NOW

"I made a promise," Becky Rant says.

She could be talking into the void. She's not completely sure.

She's been trapped in this damn room for an hour—maybe more, maybe less. Hard to tell.

The silence is deafening.

The beige is crushing.

The blandness of the room doesn't help ease the escalating feeling that everything is rapidly caving in on her. The walls feel tight. Feels like an elephant is wiping its feet on her chest. The steel cuff that's clamped around her ankle doesn't give her much of a radius to play around with. It's secured by a rusty chain attached to a chair that's been bolted to the floor of this beige-colored hell room.

A room designed, chosen for a specific purpose, she thinks.

She can't help but notice a shower-like drain in the middle of the floor. Installed for easy cleanup, she assumes, rather than think about why it's needed.

A small black speaker rests in the middle of the gunmetal-gray table in front of her. Scratches and thick cuts pepper the cool metal surface of the table. Becky Rant imagines someone clawing at the table. She's been here long enough for her brain to kick into overdrive. There's been a series of imaginary scenes bouncing around in her switchblade mind. Scenes range from a woman's nails scratching the steel table while in the throes of the sweet agony of orgasm, to someone being beaten to death, with the claw marks being the last scratches in a fight to find freedom. Find salvation. Survival.

The black speaker has a thin, black cord that snakes off toward the far wall, where it's connected to a larger phone console. The light on the speaker is lit up blood red, letting Becky Rant know it's on and ready.

Ears are listening.

Somewhere.

Someone.

Every once in a while she'll hear some shuffling or someone clear their throat on the other end. There'll be a sharp, sudden string of silence like the mute was tapped on the other end, then seconds later there'll be another noise. A cough or some other nonsense. They want her to know they are there, but they haven't said a word on purpose.

The illusion of control, she thinks. *No, not an illusion.* She knows they are in complete control.

She has tried to open a dialogue with them. Multiple times.

They aren't interested.

The *they* could be a few folks. Since Becky Rant has been sitting here, she's run through that list and narrowed it down considerably. She's had time to get herself together. Gather her fuzzy thoughts. Her dulled recall. It has been a scramble the last few days, to put it mildly.

Becky Rant's eyes scan the bare walls, searching for something to work with. There's not much to speak of. She studies the corners, the outline of the door without a knob, the square of black glass in the wall in front of her. It's the obligatory two-way glass. She's seen it before. It's there so her captors can get a nice look at her, study her like a zoo animal. She pictures them in lab coats with clipboards. They probably aren't, but it keeps the mood light for her.

Becky Rant is not unfamiliar with people wanting to look at her.

Happens a lot in her everyday life.

She imagines slowly rising from this cold, steel chair, ripping its legs free from the floor, snapping the chain that binds her, and humming the chair toward the glass like a hammer wielded by the gods. Correction. By the Goddess Becky Rant, summoner of anarchy, deliverer of wise-ass words, daughter of... someone she's never met. This goddess-hammer fantasy is so vivid she can almost hear the glass tinkle to the concrete floor upon impact. The frozen looks on the terror-stricken faces of the *they* beyond the glass.

She smiles.

She knows they will talk to her, eventually.

They're just being difficult.

"I won't hurt you. Truly I won't." She leans in, bouncing her eyebrows with some flair. "You won't feel a thing. Killing you painless-like will be my special project, but only if you let me go. You hearing me, sweethearts?"

She hears what sounds like a snicker over the speaker.

Becky Rant smiles, runs her tongue across her teeth, then leans back, slumping down in the chair. "You're such a bucket of shit."

She's hoping to draw a reaction from them.

Anything to help her narrow the list further.

Pausing, she stares at the glass, catching a slight reflection of herself. She's surprised she hasn't noticed this until now. More surprised how good she actually looks right now, considering all that's happened. Sure, there are some cuts and scrapes. Some wounds that are shutting down as the blood begins to dry, holding back the bloodgates. The aches and bruises she feels, for sure. She'll feel more later, no doubt, but it's not until you see yourself that you truly realize what you've been through. She's thankful her fiery red hair, soul-stopping blue eyes and natural appearance that most people consider attractive are still working despite the nicks and dents. Her big brain and weaponized wits are still around as well. That much she knows for a fact.

Charm, looks and a razor-sharp tongue plays in this life.

All she's ever had.

All she really needs.

She stands up, taking advantage of the foot and a half of play her ankle cuff chain allows her. A biting pain rockets up her knee as she straightens her leg, but she fights not to show it.

Not to them.

Never show that you're hurt.

"I get it," Becky Rant says. "You're not happy with me. That's fine. Not really all that happy with you, either."

She wants them to think she's sure who they are. She's not, but selling lies is one of the few weapons she holds at the moment.

More quiet.

The buzzing silence booms.

"It's been a rough ten days, hasn't it?" a woman's voice asks from the speaker.

Becky Rant stops, frozen in place.

A woman?

Not what she was expecting at all. It's a voice she doesn't recognize. Of course, the woman's voice is being run through some kind of vocal modifier, but there's no doubt in her mind that it is indeed a female. It's got this "terrorist being interviewed on a TV news magazine" robotic feel to it.

"Come on in and I'll tell you all about it, gorgeous," she says, taking a seat.

"I'm fine where I am," the robotic-sounding woman says. "Tell us a story."

Becky Rant shoots the black glass the finger.

"Come on now. You're better than that," Robot Woman says.

Becky shakes her head while looking away, lowering

her finger and placing her palms flat on the table. Fingers spread wide. She can't believe this. Defeat isn't her thing. She breathes in deep, assesses her place in life—her place in this room—then exhales big and twists her hair around her finger.

Staring into the glass at herself, Becky Rant works through the math of the situation she's in. Plays around with the shitty numbers this moment in her life has provided for her.

It's an unbalanced equation at best.

"Please," Robot Woman repeats with a lifeless tone, "tell us a story."

"Fine, gorgeous." Becky Rant shrugs her shoulders. "But let's be clear on this one thing. I'm keeping my damn promise."

Her knuckles give the horrific appearance of raw hamburger meat.

The blood smeared across them shines like black hills under the dashboard lights.

Becky Rant's hair is half wet, half dry, firing off in fifty different directions. A deranged troll doll with after-sex hair. She might have popped a rib. Fairly sure she did something to her knee. There's sand in her underwear, that much is certain. She hasn't seen a soul in miles. It's pitch-black outside, only the stars poking pinholes of light across the big Texas sky to keep her company. Becky Rant is driving like a maniac, speedometer pegged to the high eighties and the radio cranked at twenty. The Yeah Yeah Yeahs are laying down throat-ripping anthems for her to scream along with, and despite her appearance, despite her searing pain, she couldn't be happier.

Box number one checked, she thinks.

No turning back.

The energy of opportunity.

An odd pulse of manic-calm rumbles through her. A cut above her eyebrow seeps out thick, dark crimson. It's annoying the hell out of her, and she keeps dabbing the wound with a fast-food napkin she found stuffed in the glove box. Her hands are swelling. She feels them ballooning up and out on top of her bones. The chunks and slices that are cut into her knuckles sting like a bitch, but she's pushing all that unpleasantness away while enjoying the road and the tunes. The night, the spike of freedom, it's damn intoxicating. She lets the excitement of starting something new, starting something right, take hold of her.

More like, she's loving leaving something in her rearview.

Miles and miles behind her.

She checks and rechecks her old-school, gas-station highway map. She can't use a phone for directions; she's off the grid now. She estimates via the folds in the map that she's about twelve miles out. Glances at the clock. It's a little after eleven at night.

"Should be fine," she says to herself.

Her eyes slip from the clock to the dark highway, then to the passenger seat.

There's a brown bag riding shotgun. A brown bag that's clinking and rattling, as the glass bottles inside protest the speed and the occasional bump in the road.

Becky Rant's eyes drift from the seat back to the road, then immediately back to the bag.

She's been good. She's off the bottle now, needs to keep her act tight. Now more than ever. Things have changed for her recently. Adulting is no longer a distant concept, but a firm reality. Something she needs to think more about. Also, no drinking and driving.

Well, she took a snort of sauce when she got into the car, but that was to take the edge off, dull some of the immediate pain so she could drive. She was a mess when she started this trip, so that little nip was a public service rather than a weak moment of self-indulgence. But damn those bottles look nice as hell. That bag hugging the curves of the bottles like a sexy brown cocktail dress. Some nice-ass bottles of Dewer's are simply resting, waiting for her. Underutilized. Lonely. They're screaming for her. Screaming, "Drink me, sweet baby!"

Not yet, my darlings. Perhaps later. Mama's still got some work to do.

She knows she'll have to bend her sobriety to do what she needs to do. She'll have to table newfound responsibility for now so she can do what needs to be done.

A last hurrah, she told herself. *A victory lap of sorts.*

Her hand leaves the steering wheel, shaking as she fights the incredible urge to throw back a bottle. She thinks better of it, returns her hand back to complete the ten and two on the wheel. Becky Rant pops the cap on her bottle of pills instead. It contains a pharmaceutical playlist of sorts. At her worst, she was taking down a handful of Percocet, two or three OxyContin, fifteen to twenty Soma (a muscle relaxant), and a baker's dozen of Xanax twice a day. She knows how bad it got. She's not proud of it, but she owns it.

It was a gift.

A present from Ronald Church.

The math is hard, but necessary. A balancing act of pills. A continuous equation in order to mute the noise of her life, keep it all between the lines of reality. The sweet spot between functional consciousness and the hyper-numbness of bliss. She came off that regimen recently, recognizing that she was slipping, letting the pills and booze dull her edge. She'd been asleep at the proverbial wheel and let things slide, allowed herself to slip into the abyss. A place Ronald Church wanted her. A place she can no longer reside.

There was an intervention of sorts recently.

Recently meaning within the last few days.

The pills were making her sloppy. Needy. Sloppy and needy do not mix well in the life and times of Becky Rant, so she's made some rather massive changes *recently*. Now, the problem is she's currently in a ton of pain and needs to hit Texas harder than hell. She needs to be on.

Really on.

Dead on.

Charming as hell on.

The kind of *on* that requires her edges to not only be smoothed over but completely removed, set on fire, and left on the side of the highway. She did, however, think this through before leaving and only took with her what pills she deemed as necessary. If needed, she's allowed one Perc, half an Oxy, and a couple of Somas (hard to get the count right in the dark car while driving eighty plus). She's completely laid off the Xanax. Her plan is to wean herself off slowly through the duration of what is about to happen. None of this is going to be easy. Easy, unfortunately, is a rearview type of concept.

Throwing back her head, she takes down some pills with a swig of Dr. Pepper.

She loves Dr. Pepper, hasn't had one in years.

"Heads Will Roll" booms, straining the speakers. Becky Rant closes her eyes, then flips them wide open, as if her brain has just come back online. Her pupils flare, knowing, anticipating the soon-to-be dissolved goodness of big pharma that will soothe her busted body and troubled mind. Her wide eyes now allow a view, a small window, into the raging forest fire going on behind those stunning baby blues. As she grips the wheel tight in her battered hands, she wails the lyrics like a war cry. She beats her palms hard on the steering wheel despite the pain. She feels herself coming together despite the hurt.

Wrong.

It's *because* of the hurt.

She faked her own death sixteen hours ago in Los Angeles, California, and now has a stolen BMW pegged at eighty-plus miles an hour, eight miles outside of Rough Creek, Texas.

Becky Rant is locked and loaded.

YEARS AND YEARS AGO

They are young.

Troubled as hell, but still, they are young.

The three of them were joined together by a set of unfortunate circumstances that most will never know. Or understand. Frequent flyers in the Los Angeles Department of Children and Family Services, their years spent bouncing from home to home and in and out of the foster care system has forged something undefined. Something tougher than hell.

Though they cling to one another as if dumped on the lone raft that's fallen from a sinking ship, they are far too cool to openly admit how much they need each other. Not something that's in their DNA. Never once do they talk about their parents. Not only the parents who have taken them in—some good, some not so good—

but the three of them never discuss their biological parents either. Not once. Consider it a waste of time. They leave that subject for themselves. Something to grind on that will never smooth. Wounds that will never heal that they can open up, pick at, during their quiet moments alone. Something to let burn.

They stick to the things in life that teenagers talk about: sex, drugs, rock 'n' roll, then more sex. Those are at the top of their chat lists.

As it should be.

Becky Rant balls up her fist, taking a respectable swing at the much larger teenage boy's head. He bobs, swatting it away effortlessly.

"Awful," he says.

"Dick," Becky Rant says, throwing another.

This one lands with a thick pop of skin. Becky Rant raises her arms in the air like the heavyweight champion of the world, then high-steps across the empty construction site. She barely hurt Johnny, but she'll take the victories where she can. Isabel cheers from her seat on top of a stack of wood.

Johnny grabs her arms, spinning her around like a rag doll. He swings a large fist with all he has. It was agreed that he wouldn't hold back this time. They've been working on the basics for a while. Becky Rant ducks and weaves, pivots, lands a jab to his kidney, then a foot to his knee. Johnny's leg folds under him. Becky Rant gets greedy, tries to kick him in the face.

She knows it's a mistake the second she does it.

Johnny wraps his hands around her foot, twisting her to the ground. Isabel holds her breath. She fights the urge to get up and help. They agreed it was one-on-one, for now. Isabel pushes herself back down.

Johnny grits his teeth as he stands.

Becky Rant bounces up to her feet. She doesn't blink as she lands two quick right jabs to his face. As she feels his nose crack, sees the blood spill, she pulls back.

Johnny doesn't.

He wraps his thick hands around her throat, pressing harder and harder, waiting for her to tap out. Becky Rant's face moves through all the reds while her arms and hands slap and claw at his arms as he holds her.

"Give it up," he begs her.

She blows him a kiss.

He can't help but smile.

"Johnny," Isabel calls out, not liking this. She knows Becky Rant won't quit. They've been through this before.

He releases her neck, letting her body wilt to the dirt. She heaves in and out as her lungs fight for air.

"You can't let someone get ahold of you like that.

Not someone bigger than you. Do whatever you can to keep them off you."

Becky Rant coughs and gags, lies there thinking about what he said. Then she pulls herself up to her feet, spits something out, then shoots him the finger.

Her name is Rebecca, but Becky Rant is what she likes to be called. It's a nickname a foster mom gave her when she was ten years old because of Becky's ability to go off at any moment. Becky Rant is a redhead filled with mischief-fueled energy bordering on criminal. Equipped with eyes that can level you without an ounce of effort. She can also level you, as in put you in the dirt, at the flick of switch. Her anger is always at her fingertips. At the ready. Someone told her once she's a *ready, fire, aim* type of person. An indiscriminate cannon of sorts. Becky Rant liked the sound of that. She's lost count of the number of boys she's dated. Boys she's kicked the hell out of. The number of homes she's been removed from.

Reviewing any of that doesn't interest her much.

The two people she's hanging with are her family.

Her real one walked away from her before she could speak.

Isabel and Johnny are all she's got.

Isabel is a raven-haired goddess, and she has the brains to run a hedge fund.

His actual name is Jonathan, but he goes by Johnny. Don't call him Jonathan, please, he hates it. Becky Rant and Isabel assume that's what his real dad called him, but they're not sure.

Johnny's a wall of muscle, strong as a linebacker, yet kind and gentle. Big and cute, but more big brother than someone they would be involved with in a romantic sort of way. He's cool with that. Girls love him, and he enjoys his role as brother to Becky Rant and Isabel. Takes a huge amount of pride in it, actually. He's watched over them. Showed them how to fight. How to not be messed with and what to do when they are. While he is kind and caring, make no mistake, he can be brutal at times. A trigger waiting, at times dying, to be pulled.

They like to think they've watched over him too. Kept him out of more trouble than he'd care to admit. Showed him how to use emotions rather than be a slave to them. Bottle up rage and release it when needed. Use it like fuel. The three of them have fought the streets of Los Angeles and have lost more than they've won, but they do have one another. That's gotten them through this hardscrabble life they never asked for.

Johnny and Isabel help brush off her t-shirt and jeans. Isabel licks her thumb, trying to work some sludge from Becky Rant's forehead. Becky Rant wipes the blood from under Johnny's nose. They'll get cleaned up better at the filthy burger joint down the road. The type of place that doesn't ask questions, but knows how to sling grease in a proper fashion. Becky Rant and Isabel lifted a couple of bills off a douche at a westside coffee place while he argued with the minimum wage barista. They dropped a five in the tip jar, kept the pair of twenties for themselves.

They were a family.

Right or wrong.

For better or worse.

Bruised and broken in places, sure, but a family all the same.

10 DAYS AGO (ROUGH CREEK, TEXAS)

Stumbling into the Rattle Battle Bar just after eleven, Becky Rant scans the joint with red spiderweb-streaked eyes blazing.

She parked the BMW out front among the new trucks and beat-up late model Toyotas and Hondas, leaving the bottles and pills behind. Half expects them and/or the car to be gone when she leaves this dump.

The crowd looks a little thin tonight.

The heads that are available all turn, looking in her direction. All holding their eyes on her. Men and women alike unapologetically getting their fill to the point of being uncomfortable. Despite her somewhat battered appearance, she is something to see. She did the best she could to pull herself together in the parking lot before she came in, meaning she licked her fingers and finger-combed her hair. Also checked to make sure there was nothing in her teeth. Even with her usual pause-and-gawk good looks currently muted, she's still not the type of woman who normally strolls into the Rattle Battle Bar on a random weekday evening.

Any evening, really.

She's an attractive woman, that's hard to argue, but attractive in a very specific way. Fit, but not an underwear model. Cheekbones to kill for, along with the aforementioned hair and eyes that have tossed her in and out of more trouble than she'd care to mention. Becky Rant gets mistaken for an actress on some TV show all the time. She laughs it off, then uses it to her advantage later. Every year she checks to make sure that show was picked up for another season. Ratings were down last season, sweated that one out, but it thankfully got picked up again, and the constant playing in syndication doesn't hurt. Becky Rant knows when that actress hits the unemployment line she's in deep doo-doo. Of course, she knows she can work the male species even without any similarity to a hot actress, but it does, without question, help ease the workload.

Seated in the back corner of the Rattle Battle Bar sits another someone who looks out of place. A man.

A rather handsome man.

Becky Rant's eyes stop upon landing squarely on

him. She dials in. He's the only one in the bar not staring at her. The handsome man is staring deeply into the bottom of a drink. Which is unfortunate, because he's the only one she wants looking at her.

Box number two that needs to be checked.

A major part of the plan.

The plan, one might say.

The pills are starting to go to work. So are the slugs of Dewar's she took down in the parking lot. She felt she owed it to herself. A reward for a long haul, a long trip and a strange-as-hell kind of day. The room tilts ever so slightly as she zeroes in on the handsome fella in the back of the bar. She squints, fighting back the fuzzy creeping around the corners of her vision.

He's sitting alone in a beaten-up booth with tears in the red vinyl and stuffing coming out like fluffy white gore from a wound. There are several dead soldier beer bottles and an almost empty glass of brown liquor between his fingers.

Whiskey, she hopes.

Her knees give slightly. It's not him. She's not all weak-in-the-knees for this guy; she's not the sort. He's cute, but he ain't that damn cute, and Becky Rant doesn't go wobble-knees over anyone. No, it's the mix of the damn pills and sauce that has her limbs all wonky. The thought crosses her mind that she'd been off the pills for a few days and that might have cut into her tolerance. As if she hit the gym after a long layoff and tried to pick up where she left off without adjusting for the time off. She imagines her body is saying, *Oh, we're doing this shit again?*

Her head bobs a bit.

She needs to sit down before she falls down. Most of the staring faces have stopped the full-on gawking. Now it's only the men who steal the occasional glance, and do so with as much subtlety as a mating rhino.

She clings to the bar like a child holding on to the side of the pool while learning to swim. Hides it well, still looks cool, not her first rodeo, but inside she knows this situation is going south in a hurry.

Damn pills.

Damn booze.

Damn Becky Rant.

She makes a mental note to rework the dose. Lower it even more. Tomorrow is a new day, she tells herself. All is not lost, but if this is going to work out she needs to tighten herself up, and being slot-slinging blotto is not going to put Humpty Dumpty back together again. She gets mad at herself. This is a symptom of a much bigger issue. She's been sloppy, letting weakness seep into her life, weakness that didn't exist before, and it must end now. Now more than ever. She's always drank, but the pills didn't start until—

"You okay, sexy girl?"

Becky Rant turns, finding a fossil of a woman working the bar in front of her. She's tall, head full of gray with streaks of purple slicing through, and glasses thicker than gas station security glass. She's got a black duck tat on her neck and the word *love* inked on the top of one hand and *joy* on the other. Fossil Woman looks her over. There's an uncertainty in her stare, as if looking at a square peg that's wandered into a bar full of round landing spots.

"Dewar's and a glass of water, please." Becky Rant squints, looking over the tats.

Fossil Woman nods then shuffles down to the other end of the bar while keeping one eye on her.

Becky Rant checks the back corner and her handsome, lonely man. He's gone. Table empty.

"What the hell?" she whispers.

Pushing away from the bar hard, she slams into him.

The handsome stranger braces for impact. Doing his best to protect his drink and hold her shoulders. More like, trying to hold her up. She takes inventory of his dark hair, kind eyes, and even kinder face. He's no pretty boy, he's got nicks and scars, but he too is specifically attractive.

She's seen the pictures and heard the stories about him, but when this guy is this close, she gets it. Everything she's heard is true. A part of her hopes everything she's heard isn't true. She hopes she can get what she needs from him.

"You okay?" he asks.

"No."

He nods as if he knows the feeling, then tips an imaginary cowboy hat in her direction. As he leans her gently against the bar he finishes his drink then slides his empty glass onto the bar. She tries to say something snappy, but nothing worth a damn is coming to her. She can only watch him slip out the front door and into the night. A twinge of anger spikes inside her. She's mad at herself. She missed an opportunity. Not sure she has many to waste.

She rubs a silver pendant that hangs from a chain around her neck. It's half of a heart that's been cut in two, with a phrase of some kind seemingly split down the middle. The half that hangs from her neck is the left side of the heart and has the engraving BE then BIT below it. The missing right side completes the heart and the phrase. Something a young girl might wear. A friendship necklace, perhaps.

"He's hot as hell, right?"

Becky Rant turns around to find Fossil Woman has

returned with her Dewar's and a somewhat clean glass of water with something floating in it.

"If you're into that kinda of thing." She throws back the Dewar's then pushes the questionable water away from her. "Sexy Boy got a name?"

"Henry. People call him Hank, I hear. Quiet dude, hasn't been around too long. Drinks. Keeps to himself."

"Yeah? What does he do?"

"Runs a small motel off the highway. Not much to speak of. Teenagers and cheating spouses go there to hump it out mostly."

"Sounds charming."

"It's not bad. Done both."

Becky Rant nods. She spins her finger in the air, signaling for another round. Weakness is all dressed up and looking to hit the town. Besides, this woman seems to have some info that could possibly help. Fossil Woman pours her a fresh one, then drinks straight from the bottle. Becky Rant can't help but giggle. The ridiculousness of the situation is getting the best of her.

All of it.

What's happened.

Where she is in life and why.

Not to mention how she got here.

It's crazy if she breaks it all down. Almost too much to take in.

Her laughter increases. Tears roll down her red cheeks. Fossil Woman laughs along with her. Booming laughter, even if she's not sure why. Wicked-witch, cackle-like sounds rolls from Fossil Woman's toothless mouth before she takes another deep pull from the bottle. Becky Rant has her palms flat on the bar now, bracing herself as her whole body shakes while the earthquake of hysterical laughter ripples through her.

"I'm losing it." Becky Rant barely gets the words out between the hard laughs and even harder breaths of much-needed oxygen. "I'm really starting to snap."

"That's cool, darling. Lost my shit back in the early eighties," Fossil Woman blurts out, seconds away from peeing her pants.

Becky Rant has graduated to silent laughter. Her mouth wide. Face red as hell. Eyes wide as pies with tears rolling down. She begins to sweat. *Sweat?* She doesn't sweat. The room tilts even more, accelerating in speed, almost reaching a sideways view of the world.

"Wait." She holds up a finger to Fossil Woman. "Something's—"

Becky Rant's face bounces off the bar as her knees finally give out from under her.

"Wrong," Fossil Woman blurts out, rolling back into hysterics.

Becky Rant wakes up laid out on a couch.

She cracks one eyelid open.

Doesn't like what she's finding.

The couch is long past its prime, if it ever had one, with cigarette burns and dark stains of unknown origin scattered across the tattered terrain of its cheap upholstery. Perched on the arm on other side of the couch is a wiry stick of a boy. A man, in the legal sense, saddled with the look of a not-so-smart boy. Tatted sleeves cover his boney arms, spreading all the way up his shoulders to his muted jawline. He sits on the armrest, silently staring at her like a hillbilly gargoyle. His stare is creepy. A hard, emotionless gaze that's locked in dead on her.

Who is this guy?

And exactly how long has he been there?

The sun cuts through the thin lace curtains, creating thick then thin shafts of light illuminating runways of filthy clothes scattered about the room amongst the beer cans and half-eaten bags of chips. Becky Rant is pretty sure there's a pile of chicken bones sitting in the seat of a brown, fake-leather recliner.

Smacking her lips together, she fights to find some moisture inside her mouth. Turning her head slightly to the right, she sees Fossil Woman sitting in a busted-up chair about a foot and a half from the couch. She's staring at Becky Rant as well, a slight grin spread across her face and a shotgun resting in her lap. Becky Rant looks between the two of them, then at the shotgun.

How long have I been here?

Have they been watching me sleep?

And what the hell's with the shotgun?

She quickly looks under the ratty blanket that's covering her to make sure she's dressed. She is. Also, she seems to be unharmed or messed with. She breathes a small sigh of relief. It's a little early in the day for Becky Rant to beat someone to death.

Not too early, but still early.

An old clock ticktocks loudly on the living room wall nestled between a mounted deer head and a big-mouthed fish that have both seen better days. Becky Rant pushes herself up onto her elbows, surveying the situation. Searching her brain for the right words to say. On the wall to the left of her is a massive, cast-iron Jesus on the cross. She glances to Jesus, then back to her new friends. Wiry Stick Boy and Fossil Woman's eyes never leave her.

The clock ticks.

Becky Rant eyes the door, then the clock. It's a little after ten in the morning. She assumes her car is back at the bar. She hopes the car is back at the bar. She has work to do, no time for whatever this is.

"So," she finally says, breaking the blistering silence. "Thank you for letting me crash—"

Wiry Stick Boy drops down from his perch onto the couch with a bounce. His face never alters from its creepy, pre-sexual assault state. Becky Rant's head tilts, birdlike. Balls her fists. Cocks her knee slightly, ready to strike full throttle with a kick if needed.

The clock tocks.

Fossil Woman still hasn't said anything, but she does clear some phlegm from her throat. It takes some time. She shifts in her chair, adjusting the shotgun slightly.

Becky Rant hates to admit it, but she's woken up in worse situations.

Wiry Stick Boy scoots closer to her on the couch, his hip now touching her toes. She fights a shiver. He lifts up the blanket, revealing her bare feet.

She sits up straight, looking around the room. "Where the hell are my shoes?"

Wiry Stick Boy softly pinches her pinkie toe with his thumb and finger. "This little piggy..." His creepy vibe has moved up the charts with a bullet.

"Okay now, Skinny," Becky Rant says. "Let's not—"

"She's pretty, Mama." He looks to Fossil Woman, his face lifeless. "Damn she's pretty."

"Sure. Sure she is. Pretty girl." Shifts her shotgun again. "Doesn't look like she's from around here, does she?"

"Nope," he says, leering. "Kinda like it."

Becky Rant's body goes tight.

"Looks like someone from out of town. Way out of town." Fossil Woman stabs her tongue into her cheek then says, "Like some girl from California maybe, given the looks of her sweet ass, the car and the plates."

He nods.

The clock ticktocks.

"Wait a second," Becky Rant says. "I just stopped here—"

"You with them?" Fossil Woman chirps.

"Who?"

"Those bikers. The ones from California. Tell 'em we don't do that business no more at the bar. That was a one-time thing."

Wiry Stick Boy looks away for the first time. Picks at his nails.

"Listen to me." Becky Rant leans in. "I don't know what you're talking about. I'm just a girl passing through."

Becky Rant eyes the shotgun, then the door. She's got no idea where her shoes are. She does the quick analysis on the time it will take for her to put a foot into Wiry Stick Boy's face, then wrestle the shotgun loose from granny's grip, or at least knock her down long enough to get to the door without catching some lead in the spine.

Wiry Stick Boy readies his finger-thumb pincher, about to snag another one of her toes.

"Don't." Becky Rant lowers her chin. "One warning. One only."

He giggles, snagging her big toe with a hard pinch.

Becky kicks him in the throat, flinging the blanket up and over Fossil Woman's head in a single move. Slight alteration to the original analysis she made, but it's working. Wiry Stick Boy grabs his throat, unable to breathe, leaning over choking, gagging for his life. She gives him a hard jolt with the ball of her foot. A popping crack to his jaw sounds off, mixed with the ticking of the clock. It was more to move him off the couch than anything else, but she'll gladly take any pain it's causing him.

Fossil Woman stands up, looking like an angry ghost, the blanket covering her head, swinging wildly around, trying to free herself.

Becky Rant springs up from the couch, scans quickly for her shoes.

Nowhere to be found.

"What the hell?" she mutters to herself as she bolts to the door. Something else is off. Reaching, searching around her neck, her fingers come up empty. The silver half-heart on a chain is missing. "Shit."

She's got no time.

"Damn." Wiry Stick Boy gags. "Dammit."

Fossil Woman has spun free from her blanket prison and levels her shotgun on Becky Rant, who's hauling ass toward the door.

"Stop goddammit!"

Becky Rant gets one hand on the doorknob and shoots them the finger with her free hand. Throwing open the door, the blast of heat and sunlight almost knocks her over, coupled with a wave of crushing nausea from her night out on the town. As she leaps, clearing the steps, she hears the pump of the shotgun behind her. She braces herself for the sound of the door exploding. For the coming boom of a bursting confetti-bomb made of wood and glass.

But it never comes.

Instead, she only hears the sound of her own labored breath.

Then Wiry Stick Boy calls out from the door. "Bitch."

"Good God," Becky Rant blurts out to herself.

She runs hard, legs churning, knees pumping. Bare feet slapping the pavement harder and harder. The yelps and calls from Fossil Woman are indecipherable, trailing off as Becky Rant puts some quality distance between her and that house. All the while, she's calculating the range of that shotgun. She's no stranger to being shot at. Doesn't happen every day, mind you, but it's happened more than once, and it doesn't take double-digit run-ins with guns to become a quick study in time and distance.

A new to-do list also begins to form in her mind. A subset of the original. The living document that her plans have become.

One: Get away from that house.

Two: Find her car. Guessing it's back at the bar.

Three: Find that charming lady-killer—

"Problems?"

She whips her head around. The lady-killer himself, Hank, is running next to her. He's more equipped for the run than Becky Rant, however, wearing what the well-dressed workout warrior wears these days. Tight microfiber black stuff that hugs his body, baggy white shorts and slick, black runner's shoes. She catches herself zeroing in on the sweat on his tanned skin. His perfect jawline. His chest. Arms. As much as she likes the view, she can't ignore her own bare-ass feet. She's having the hardest time looking away from the shoes. Imagines they are like running on pillows of chilled lamb's wool.

"Slight issue, yes," she gets out between breaths.

"Glenda?"

"Who?"

"Her." Hank thumbs behind him. "The bartender and her son."

"Oh. Yeah, them. They do that a lot?"

"I've heard stories. Chatter at the coffee shop. Some dirty business they've got going on. I should have said something to you last night."

"What the hell?"

"I know." He extends a bouncing hand. "Hank."

She shakes it while running full tilt, knowing damn well who he is.

"Rebecca." She doesn't know why she got all proper with the name. She shakes her head. "Becky Rant works."

"Becky Rant? All together?"

"Yeah. Becky Rant."

"Well, all right then. Becky Rant it is." He lets the rhythm of their strides fill the conversational dead air.

"I'm all for a good run, Becky Rant, but do you mind if we slow the pace a bit?"

She realizes they've been running, sprinting really, as if they were being chased by a bear. She looks to him. They share a quick laugh, slowing down to a reasonable pace. After a minute or two of silent jogging, she places a hand on his arm.

"Can we stop for a second?"

They're in the middle of a neighborhood street. Not your typical suburban area. There are no McMansions here. Most of the houses date back to the seventies, and haven't seen much in the way of remodeling since then. Most do, however, have new trucks in the driveway. Big, shiny ones. Some go with the Ford, while others wave the Chevy flag. Becky Rant imagines the old men in coffee shops arguing over which is superior while offering their take on politics and local gossip.

She's no stranger to small-town life. No stranger to the mindset of generational lower income. Deep pride in what you have, disdain for what you don't, and an even-deeper disdain for those who have more than you. Decent people. Work hard. No money. Little hope. Little future. That's what she remembers about that life, and she has no intention of repeating it.

"I need to find my car." She quickly removes her

hand from his arm, realizing she's left it there for at least a full three or four Mississippis.

"That it?" Hank points about a block over.

She shakes her head. Only in a town like this would the local bar be across the street from a church and a block over from a neighborhood filled with families. Fairly sure she saw a preschool not far from here either.

"Thanks." Her feet are killing her.

Now that she's stopped, the pavement is feeling hotter than hell, the concrete searing the soles of her feet. Hank reads her discomfort, takes in the features of her face, cracks a grin and escorts her off the street and onto a shaded lawn. The cooler grass feels like heaven on her pavement-baked soles.

He saw her the second she walked into the bar last night. She's hard to miss, especially around here. If he's being honest, she's hard to miss in most places. Sure, it's the way she looks, but there's also something to the way she moves. The way she carries herself. There's attitude, to be sure, but there's something intriguing and very familiar at the same time. He doesn't know her, but she seems like someone he would. Maybe this town is taking hold of him. Grabbing ahold of his thinking. Well, he knows it has, but that doesn't change the fact she's the most interesting thing that's bumped into him in some time.

Easy, he tells himself, noticing that he's staring into those blue traps she calls eyes.

"You okay?" he asks. "You good now?"

She throws him a look. *Are you kidding me?*

"Well." He nods, acknowledging the strangeness of the situation. "Better at least?"

"Yeah." She checks her pockets, making sure the BMW fob is still there. "Just need to find a place to stay for a couple of days." She says it as if she didn't know he made his meager living managing a place down the highway.

He snaps his fingers and gives her that damn smile again. "Ya know what? I know a place."

"Do you?"

"I do. Some call it the Four Seasons of Rough Creek."

"You don't say."

"I do say. Management is a little surly, but I can get you a rate."

"Oh yeah? A bed and breakfast type thing?" Trying to make it look good.

"Not quite. It's a tiny roadside motel I run. I can get you into the cleanest room, if you like."

She breathes in deep. Lets her mind unspool. Boxes are being checked, stars are aligning, but there's a nagging something tugging at her. The feeling that massive trouble is stampeding her way. The way it has most of her life. Only this trouble is in this man's smile. His eyes. Her stomach bounces. She'd call it butterflies, but that would be admitting too much. The linger of booze and pills coupled with the morning exercise has her head dipped deep into a thick soup of sorts. She knows all about this man. What he is. What he's done. But still, here she is looking at him like a goofy eighth grader.

"Sorry," Hank says, raising his hands. "Was that too—"

"No." She resets, shaking herself loose from her broken brain. "Best offer I've had in weeks."

He nods, jogs in place, then extends his arm forward asking her to take the lead.

They jog together toward the bar, Hank on the sidewalk, Becky Rant in the grass.

The motel room door swings open.

It's a dump.

That's being kind. Actually, the place aspires to be a dump. This is a certified shithole.

Becky Rant smiles, trying to hide her gag reflex.

Don't show it on your face. Don't show it on your face.

She's not very good at it.

"You don't like it?" Hank asks as his face sags.

The wood paneling is peeling away from the wall, as if it wants to leave as much as Becky Rant does. There are wide cuts and deep chunks removed from the forest-thick burgundy carpet. Like squires had a knife fight by the bed. The chair in the corner has three legs, though four are necessary for adequate seating. She's not sure how many legs the creature that's crawling on the ceiling has. Hard to tell if it's fur or legs on it. There's also a large, oddly shaped, dark, five-inch stain on the bed. Could be vomit, could be urine or blood.

Please let it be vomit.

"It's fine," she struggles to say. "This is the clean one?"

Hank looks her dead in the eye. He seems hurt. Swallows, looking away, borderline offended.

"No, this is great. Thank you for—"

Hank breaks out into laughter.

"You dick," she blurts with wide eyes and a smile.

"Sorry, that was fun. For me at least." Hank shows her out the door. "Come on."

They enter a new room a few doors down. He's right; it's not the Four Seasons, but it is light-years ahead of the room they were in moments ago. First, it is clean. The walls are painted in a soothing shade of blue. The hardwood floor looks rugged, but installed with great care and craftmanship. A thick, plush rug provides soft landing from the bed and rests in front of the TV. The chrome fixtures in the bathroom shine. The tile beams white. The bed is made up nice, with a comforter enclosed in a duvet cover that Becky Rant might consider taking with her.

Hank stands in the doorway, watching her reaction.

He's worked hard on this space. This is his vision for the rest of the rooms of the motel. Has long-range thoughts of adding a restaurant, though he's not sure that will ever happen. He can only do one thing at a time. Did the floors himself, painted the walls, remodeled the bathroom. Not a DIY guy naturally, but he's enjoyed the process of learning and working with his hands. It's provided a nice distraction for him. A sense of therapy.

She steps into the middle of the room, scanning the area while nodding. "Better," she says. "Very much better."

"Good." Hank leans in the doorway with a smile. "Glad you approve."

"You must take the real fancy room for yourself."

"Good God no." He snickers. "I'd never stay in this shithole."

She cocks her head.

Hank thumbs behind him, motioning toward the window. Up on a hill not too far in the distance is an older, two-story house. It's perched over the motel like a cozy watchtower. Grayish blue with dark trim and pillars along a wraparound porch. Victorian in style, Becky Rant thinks, and the place looks well kept. Resembles something out of a classic Southern neighborhood. It's a nice place, but there's a darkness to it. The way it sits out of the way. Up high looking over things. She half expects lightning and thunder to fire off on cue.

"You live there?" Becky Rant scrunches her nose, masking the other questions she has.

"I do. It was part of the deal when I bought the place."

She's having a hard time piecing this all together. The man she's read about and studied, coupled with what she's heard, does not fit this profile. Isabel said kind words about him, but she was blind. Hard for Becky Rant to grasp all the things swirling in her head about Hank the Lady-Killer. However, as much as she hates to admit it, after spending a few minutes with him, Becky Rant can now completely understand her friend's blindness.

There's an easiness to him wrapped up in a rugged

movie star wrapper. He speaks and moves with confidence. A person in control of cool.

"So, you'll take the room?" He holds the key out for her, its oversized forest green plastic room number dangling from the chain with a gold longhorn emblem reflecting under the light. *Of course it does*, she thinks.

She steps back, trying to shake off the weirdness of the situation. She wants to dump everything she knows out into the air. To understand. The desire to talk to him is crushing. She knows she can't. She has a plan. A promise to keep. It feels like there's something else, something she's forgetting. Pushing it down, she turns, looking around the room and nodding, accepting the strange. Lets it fade and fold into the narrative she's working.

The plan is in play.

"Not any creepy peepholes in here, right?" she asks, only half kidding.

"No." Hank steps in and shows her a mark on the wall. A rough, raised spot. Looks like it's been covered with putty and painted over. "Fixed all those."

Hank grins, leaving the key on the dresser as he steps toward the door. Becky Rant stares at the spot on the wall. Tries not to throw up. Tells herself, *at least they're fixed.* Where would we be in this life without the power of rationalization?

"Why don't you get settled?" Hank stands in the doorway. His broad shoulders shield the sun from blasting into her eyes.

Settled? Really? Haven't been settled in... ever.

"Okay. Then?" she asks.

"What?"

"What do people do around here?"

"Not much."

"That sucks."

"*Not much* is why people live here."

Becky Rant thinks on that statement, taking a seat on the bed.

"Maybe I'll let you buy me dinner," she says.

Hank stops cold. The suddenness of her dinner comment is only matched by his sudden shutdown. His expression changes. Freezes almost. His shoulders inch up closer to his ears. His spark seems to have left him in a flash. Hank the cool, the slick charmer of small-town Texas, has been wiped clean. Removed and replaced by this empty shell standing in front of her.

"Did I say something—"

"No, I just... I don't... I have something going on."

"Really? Could've sworn you said *not much* is going on."

"I said *people* don't do much around here and—"

"You're not people?"

Hank jams his tongue into his cheek, fighting a smile. It's been a while since he's sparred with someone like Becky Rant. Some time has passed since he's had to volley back and forth with someone as skilled in the give-and-take as she is. It's certainly been a while since he's done this with a woman like this. A woman like Becky Rant, who's holding his eyes the way she is at the moment.

"It's dinner, man," she says, her voice coated in candy.

He takes a deep breath. Everything inside him is screaming *NO*.

"What could go wrong?" she continues.

Everything, he thinks.

"Not that big of a deal."

This is a horrible idea.

"Is there a problem? I'm sorry if I—"

"No." He holds out a hand, asking for a moment. "Sounds fun. I'll come by around six."

"Six? What are we, eighty-two?"

"Fine. Seven?"

"Oh, now we're in our sixties. Better."

"Places around here close at nine."

"Wow." She struggles not to roll her eyes. She's forgotten all about this aspect of small-town life. "Okay, seven then."

"Good."

"Great."

An awkward, silent beat passes, like teenagers staring at one another with no idea what to do. Hank nods then leaves, shutting the door behind him.

The air conditioner kicks on.

The cool air blows across Becky Rant's face, gently flowing through her hair ever so slightly. She shakes her head back and forth like she's wandering in a spring field in a hair commercial. Closing her eyes, she lets the cool air bring her back to earth. She exhales big, willing her thoughts to collect. It's been a strange twenty-four hours or so, to put it mildly. The cool air dries the thin coat of sweat that's spread across her forehead since their little jog. She needs a shower.

She needs to think. To find her focus. Needs to get her head right.

There's still plan. A fight to fight.

A war that needs to be won.

Her eyes pop open.

Barely above a whisper, she says, "Here. We. Go."

The speaker crackles.

"Thought you were giving up the pills," Robot Woman says.

Becky Rant cocks her head. The cut above her eye is starting to bleed again.

Who is this woman?

That simple question about the pills just narrowed down the list of her captors to two. She can't remember exactly when, but she mentioned the pills, and wanting to stop them, somewhere along the way to a very specific set of someones. The identity of this woman, this Robot Woman, however, remains a mystery. She can guess. Could be a handful of skanks she's known over the years. Plenty to choose from. Plenty who would want to see her hurt or watch her die slowly. The robotic quality to her tone has completely masked anything that Becky Rant could recognize, and none of those previously mentioned skanks would be associated with the two groups Becky Rant has narrowed the list of captors down to.

"I did. I did kick the pill popping," she says, taking a seat. The chain around her ankle clinks and drags along on the floor. "Had a slight slip, okay? Ya know, it was a bit of a trying day. Is a healthy slab of compassion from that side of the speaker too much to hope for?"

Nothing from the black box resting on the table.

Becky Rant shakes her head. "This is fairly damn silly, don't ya think?"

Silence, save for the white noise buzz of the room.

"Whoever you are, whatever you are, you know damn well what happened, right? You know it all. You're just, ya know, fuckin' with me."

Nothing.

"Oh come the hell on—"

"Want to hear it from you," Robot Woman finally chimes in.

"Come in here." Becky Rant cracks a smile. "Let me see that pretty face."

"Fine where I am."

"I won't hurt you."

"Not what I've heard."

Becky Rant smiles wider now. She got something out of Robot Woman. A tiny nugget. It's not much, but Robot Woman screwed up and said something off script. The voice from the black box just moved the conversation to outside the box and confirmed that she's heard things about Becky Rant. There's a shuffle on the other end of the speaker, then the halting cut of quiet from MUTE being slapped down. Robot Woman just confirmed what Becky Rant assumed.

Whoever is behind that glass knows her history.

That potentially narrows the list to one. At the very least, it confirms the list at two. Shortens it to a much more manageable number. They know what's happened and they are either truly fuckin' with her, or they want to fill in the gaps of their Swiss cheese-like knowledgebase.

"What did you hear about me, gorgeous?" Becky Rant presses, hoping to dig a little deeper into this.

The room buzzes.

The black box stares back at her, lifeless, its burning red cyclops eye providing some limited form of personality.

"Let's hack it all up." Becky Rant points back and forth between her and the glass. "Just us girls."

More silence.

"No matter what you've heard, I won't hurt you. I

like you. Your style. It's intoxicating. I'm the one who's been hurt here. More than you'll ever know."

The speaker crackles again, but no one speaks.

Becky Rant turns, leans in, almost letting her lips touch the speaker as if whispering something intimate to a close friend.

"Give me a sign, Robot Woman," she says with a sneer. "Cluck your nasty robotic tongue twice if he's in there with you."

Nothing.

"Come on now. Talk to me, gorgeous."

Sounds like someone sighing through the speaker.

Becky Rant doesn't know exactly who's on the other end of that line—could be only this woman, could be an army of psychos—but she knows she at least has their attention. Which is more than she's had since she woke up chained to this damn chair. She's got a very strong idea of who's behind this, but she needs to be sure. She needs to stomp on the gas. Push the conversation hard while the door has been opened, even if it's only a crack. She might not get another chance like this.

Becky Rant decides to roll the dice.

"That man is garbage. You know it, I know it. He'll turn on you. Only a matter of time, if he hasn't already. Give him up. Give him up to me."

There's the faintest of sounds on the other end. A whisper maybe.

"Take the leash off of me. Let me go at that piece of shit."

Becky Rant's stare could rip the speaker in half. Her face feels like it's just caught fire. Ears burn. Her heart pounds. The simple thought of who might be behind this has her cranked three rungs up the rage ladder. She sits with eyes locked and palms flat on the cool steel of the table. Feels like she could levitate off the anger that's bubbling up inside of her. The seconds drag, feeling like hours.

"Tell us a story," Robot Woman finally says.

"Bitch."

"B itch." Becky Rant sips her coffee, looking out into her lush backyard.

A squirrel snatches yet another avocado from the tree closest to the back gate.

"Bitch," she says again, as if the squirrel can hear her.

She's tanned, rested, strong and stunning. This is Becky Rant before things went sideways.

Before her death.

Cracking her knuckles, she's reminded of her fight last night. Not a real fight, rather play fighting in the name of fitness. She's been working out with this boxing club that a friend in the LAPD got her involved in. Great workout, and it has helped her sharpen some skills. She never in her life thought she'd have police pals, but she does now. An unintended consequence from him.

Not by choice, necessarily, but they are there.

She's always been a pretty good fighter. Had to be. An older brother, well, an older dude who also lived at the home, a person she considered a brother, showed her a few things. Johnny was patient when he showed her and Isabel how to whip some ass. Some valuable street techniques. How to throw and take a punch. How to stand. Using leverage when and where she could. He died awhile ago, it escapes her how. That's not true. She remembers exactly how he died, but she chooses to bury the things she'd rather not think about. Regardless, she took his teachings to heart and then made them her own. She's added to her arsenal of ass whipping.

Being an attractive girl who was moved from home to home, from small town to small town around LA, shipped to family after family that gave up on her, made her very good with her fists. Skilled with her feet. Learned how use her knees like pistons made of concrete. Palms of her hands became sledgehammers to noses and chins. Gouging with her fingers then breaking the fingers of others. Turning anything into a weapon became a challenge. A game. She's bashed in more than a few sets of balls in her day. The way she saw it, she had only a couple of choices. She understood early on that she either had to get comfortable with getting groped by people she didn't want touching her, or she needed to get real comfortable fighting.

She likes to choose who touches her, thank you.

Nobody lays a finger on Becky Rant without losing something valuable.

Her more civilized workout is later today. This is LA after all. She sips her coffee, checks the clock. She has a little time this morning before her spin class, then it's off to yoga with the neighborhood MILFs. She needs to get dressed, although she doesn't see why she can't workout in her pink robe and puppy pajamas. There is a certain amount of social pressure to throw on the overpriced, skintight garb and show off the goods. Helps her keep everyone where they need to be. Some women love her. Some hate her. All the men at least steal a look. This is the balance Becky Rant needs. The one that's served her well in life so far.

She needs to brush her teeth too, she thinks as she runs her tongue across them.

Yeah, they need a good scrub.

She threw up about an hour ago.

It's her second day without the pills and she's fuzzy as hell. Irritable too. Her mind has drifted while staring out the window at those thieving-ass squirrels. She turns her attention back to the pad of paper she's been working on, which rests on a dark wood table. She loves that table. Took her forever to pick it out. Growing up the way she did, she never thought she'd be that kind of girl. The kind that takes weeks to pick out the perfect wood for the perfect kitchen table. Most places she grew up in didn't even have a kitchen table. Barely a functioning kitchen.

She counts there were about ten different kitchens over the course of her childhood. Remembering the kitchen layouts is easier than remembering the faces of the parents who didn't want her.

Who let her down.

Who let her go.

The pad of paper has TO-DOS across the top of the page in a peach script of sorts. Looks like the title to a really boring romance novel or a cheap wedding invitation. The paper is an off-white color with faded peachy lines for her to outline her thoughts and needs.

Her many *to-dos*.

There's a lot to cover in a short amount of time. A ton to figure out.

Usually, she uses this pad to jot down things to pick up at Ralphs or adjustments to her workout schedule or just simple reminders about dry cleaning, yard service and whatnot.

Today her to-dos are much different.

There's a ton to figure out when faking your own death.

To make things more complicated, there's the thing where he's going to try and murder her. Yes, she's sure Ronald Church is going to try and get rid of her. That creates some variables she doesn't know and can't really control. That makes this to-do exercise much more complicated. She needs to go at this from multiple angles. Multiple scenarios are possible that easily spiderweb into a thousand outcomes. Many, hell, *most* of which are not favorable to Becky Rant.

That layer of complexity adds a little something to the murder mix here. She needs to figure out how to let him think he's killed her without, of course, letting him actually end her life. She's come to grips with the idea that he's going to do it. That he wants to do it. There was a time when she had moments of panic about it, to be sure.

She cried.

She hated herself for crying about it. She dried her eyes, slapped herself, poured some Dewar's, then took a long bath, letting her brain go to work. Removing emotion is the key. Removing the pills that Ronald used to keep her pleasantly sedated was big as well. She had her cry, now she needs to work this all out. Get detailed, go brain surgeon with the thing. There's a reason surgeons don't operate on loved ones. Too personal. She doesn't have that luxury of complete separation because, in this case, she is the loved one. Still, she needs to get clinical with her thinking as much as possible.

Treat it like a puzzle.

A game.

She sips her coffee, her last permitted drug.

What's really muddying the waters is that she doesn't know exactly how he's going to do it. She has a pretty firm idea of when, at least a time frame, but the *how* is the big question. It's everything, really. She's spent the last three mornings working through this same ritual. Coffee, call a squirrel a bitch, and stare at a blank, peachy to-do pad turning over how much and how little she knows. The first day was a little emotional, but now she does her best to keep that under wraps. Tears will form and she pushes them down as hard as she can. She'll slap herself, think about taking some pills, stop herself, throw down a cocktail instead. Or beat a cop's ass at the gym. Whatever it takes to remove her emotions.

The day she realized what was happening was tough. The day you understand that someone is going to try and kill you, that's a tough one to get your mind around. Sure, people have given it a shot in the past. Becky Rant is no stranger to violence, or the angst of others, but she didn't think it would come at her from this direction.

Not from him.

Not from someone she trusted.

She's been very careful over the years not to trust too many people. Her vetting process is tight, near FBI quality, and her ability to read people is possibly one of the best in the world. But this one. This guy. He slipped through. She's good, but she hates how good he is. He tricked her into something. Many things. The type of things that cannot be forgiven or worked through. He dug in deep and pulled out everything inside of her.

All that, and then she figured out he was going to kill her.

Somewhat of a deal breaker.

She feels the tears start again. She chews on the inside of her cheek, sips her coffee, then eyeballs a butterfly outside the window. Staring, she lets the sadness drift into the background. It's a beautiful day. Most are, around here. Shame she has to spend most of the day planning her death. She's never planned a wedding, but she thinks that must be very similar to this. There's a lot to consider. Moving parts. Points of failure. Locations. Folks to keep happy.

Why did she trust him? Did she go soft? Is he really that good? There had to be signs. He's evil beyond reason. What he's done to her, to the people she cares about, and what he will do...

It needs to end.

He's going to kill you, Becky.

And you're going to let him. Kinda.

How the hell do I pull this off?

Then it hits her. She needs to control the narrative. She needs to control how and when he tries to murder her. It's the only way to push the odds of the game back to her favor.

The squirrel pops up, landing on the windowsill with half an avocado in its little claws. Its nose twitches at a thousand miles an hour as it snatches a bite while never looking away from Becky Rant. They hold one another's eyes. Dead stare. Locked. Only the glass separating their disdain. Becky Rant cracks a grin then raises her coffee, toasting the furry little thief.

"Good on you, bitch."

H ank and Becky Rant sit at a table near the back.

The place is old, the tables are beaten all to hell, but there's a charm to the joint. Becky Rant can't seem to get the balance right between the uneven legs of her chair. She did think it was sweet, borderline cool, that Hank pulled the busted chair out for her. Something she's only seen in movies, never in the real world, and certainly not done for her. She's almost ashamed how much the gesture struck her.

Never forget who this guy is.

It's only them and an elderly couple that has a taken booth near the cashier. Becky Rant steals a glance at them when she feels she can. They both sit on the same side of the booth, maybe an inch or two away from one another, but haven't said a word. Barely a glance between them. The man will pat then hold her hand every once in a while, then she'll smile.

The young waiter sets down a steaming plate of cheese-coated enchiladas, then asks if Becky Rant would like another beer. She looks to Hank, who's still nursing his first bottle. In her experience, most men are quick to order up as many drinks as possible when with her. A subtle-as-a-train-wreck method of getting her drunk in hopes of an enchanted evening. The obligatory first stop on the get-into-Becky-Rants'-pants highway. Many have tried, but only a select few have reached that destination.

Most who tried without clearance left with a limp or an extended hospital stay.

Over the years, she's learned to handle her liquor like a sailor and fight like a monster. But this one, Hank, he hasn't gone that way. He likes her, she can tell, but he hasn't been overly aggressive, or aggressive at all. He's charming as hell, always smiling and quick with a joke, but he also always puts a fair amount of distance between them during their, albeit brief, time together. Both physical and emotional. Yes, he pulled out the chair, but in a way that was a slick. Making sure he got to sit in the chair with his back to the wall.

She knew he would.

Makes him feel safe. He can see everyone without anyone getting the jump from behind.

It's what she would have done.

"You getting another one?" she asks, motioning to the waiting waiter.

"Sure." Almost sounding like he's considering it as he answers, "Two more, please."

"Actually," she cuts in, "you have good margaritas?"

The waiter nods with a shrug. He's about as exciting as growing back hair.

"You're quite a salesman. How about two of your finest margaritas?" Becky Rant says with some plastered on cheer.

"What do you think?" Hank nudges his chin toward her plate as the waiter slumps off. "Look okay?"

"Looks tasty."

"It's a good place. Aside from our boy, Sparky the Wonder Slug, a nice family runs the joint." He picks up his fork. "Don't laugh, but this is considered the *fancy Mexican place* around here."

"I get that." She nods, looking around the place. "This where you bring all the chicks?"

"No." He doesn't look up from his food.

"Aw. I'm special?"

"No," Hank says with a smile, still not looking at her.

"You are a charmer."

"I take them to the *fancy Italian place.*"

The waiter drops off two beers and three margaritas then slumps off. Becky Rant and Hank share a laugh. *The kid must have gotten confused.* She clinks her beer bottle with his, then throws back a slug. Lifting up her margarita, she swipes her tongue across the salt—makes with some eyes while she does it, of course—and sucks down some of the frozen, lumpy, green goodness through her purple straw.

"Sparky ain't much on people skills," she says, coming up for air, "but the booze is strong like bull."

Hank follows suit, taking a tongue swipe off his glass, then giving an eyebrow raised in approval.

She fork-cuts her stack of chicken verde enchiladas. The sauce shifts to the edges of the flowered plate and the cheese flows like a lumpy river of goodness. The cheese strings from her fork to her lips. Steam drifts up, warming her face.

Hank watches her, tilting his beer back. He can't help but smile. Watching her in general is enjoyable, but her struggle with the enchiladas is the real show. The cheese is never-ending, not willing to release no matter how hard she tries. It's a war of stubbornness. Hank reaches over and snaps the string with a pinch of his fingers, ending the conflict.

She gives him a thumbs-up, mouthing a silent word of thanks.

"Can I ask a stupid question?" She wipes her mouth with her napkin then pauses, trying to decide which drink in front of her to go with.

Hank pushes the margarita her way. "Can I give a stupid answer?"

"Why are you here?"

"Here?" Motions to her with smile. "I'm having a lovely dinner with a lovely person."

"No, dummy." She bites her lower lip. "This town. The motel thing. Why?"

"You not like it here?"

"That's not it. It's great. I could live without the strange-ass bartender and her creepy-ass son, but I can see some of the appeal to the town. I guess I'm wondering why a single, cute guy in his... what? Thirties? A guy like that could be anywhere, doing anything, so why is a guy like you living here?"

"Who said I'm any of those things?"

"You're not single?"

"Did you call me cute?"

"Damn. I'm not going to HR, am I?"

Hank takes a swig from his beer. It's not lost on Becky Rant that he's favoring the beer over the margarita. He's choosing the one with less alcohol. Wants to maintain control.

"I like it here," he says.

"That's it?"

"Afraid so."

Becky Rant has spent a lifetime reading people. Good people and bad. Men and women. Young and old. And right now she'll be damned if she can get a read on Henry "Hank" Kane. He does give her plenty of fun to enjoy, but nothing in the way of honesty. Not a single piece of tangible information she can sink her teeth into. In her experience, when someone is hiding the truth they clam up. Shut down. Do everything they can to avoid and evade conversation, not wanting to create an opportunity to slip up.

He's not doing that.

Does he want to let it all out, or is he as good as I've been told?

Hank is engaged and present, but he's simply offering fluff and distraction in the way of good looks and defense-melting charm. The booze isn't helping her fact-finding mission either. She should take his lead and stick with the beer. She takes another hit off the margarita. She's laid off the pills today. That might be the last of those for her. At least for a while. At this stage of the game she considers that to be true personal growth. Giving up booze and pills at the same time might be too much to ask, although she knows she will have to get better control of everything very soon.

She can't lose sight of what's at stake.

Can't let her promise fade and disappear.

"How about you?" Hank asks before forking a bite of enchilada.

"Me?"

"Yes, you." He pauses, chews, then points his fork. "What brings Becky to this dead-end town?"

"Never said *dead-end*—"

"It was implied." A swig of beer. "Or is that your thing? Travel to a random Texas town. Find a bar. Drink yourself blind—"

"Hey, there were pills involved."

"Even better." He's enjoying this. He leans in. "You get bored, pop some pills, head east to Texas, then drink until you stumble home with an elderly psychotic bartender and her slow-witted son."

Becky Rant leans back in her seat, cradling her margarita like it contains a rare magical elixir rendered by the gods. Her eyes flare. A smile spreads. It's been a long time since she's enjoyed the company of someone like this. Planning your death can be draining. Here, in this one-gas-station town in the middle-of-nowhere Texas at this off-the-map Mexican joint, is the first man she's wanted to spend time with in she doesn't know how long. She can't release her stare on him.

Her minds snaps back into place, recalling what she knows about him and what he's done. What she's done. She remembers her plan.

Putting her drink down, she clears her throat. "What're you running from, Hank Kane?"

Hank squints, not sure he told her his full name. "You tell me first, Becky."

"Becky Rant. Friends call me Becky Rant." She can't remember if she told him that or not.

"Sorry, right. Becky Rant."

She takes a bite.

He sips his beer.

Eyes fire off between them.

Becky Rant decides it's time to move down the to-do list.

"So." She leans forward, carefully setting her fork down. "You going let me see the big house on the hill tonight?"

"What?"

"Oh, you want to grab a six-pack and hang out in my room? I hear that's how things go around there. High school style. That could be fun."

Hank begins shutting down again like he did back at the motel. His expression drops. It's like he's become small, a reduction of himself. All the charm and life leaves him in an instance, as if a plug has been pulled from a drain, the fun energy that seemed limitless moments ago drained away from him.

Becky Rant can't fully process what she's seeing. It's all over his face. Something is wrong.

"Did I say something?"

He looks away, trying to get the waiter's attention.

"Is everything okay?"

Hank gives the signal for the check.

"Hank?" She tries to touch his hand.

He pulls back. "I'm fine. It's okay." Still avoiding eye contact. "I've got a long day tomorrow, got to get up early, so we should probably head back."

"Oh, okay."

"You done with your food. Is that alright?"

"I guess so." She picks up her purse, trying to find some form of cool.

The waiter drops off the check, then attempts to leave the table. Hank puts his hand out, stopping him while slipping him a few twenties, not bothering to check the bill. Not caring if he's overpaying.

The mood of the table has shifted so hard, so suddenly, Becky Rant can't even begin to understand what has happened. There was an air of playful seduction. Like school kids flirting, only they are not kids.

There's no need to play games as she saw it. They are adults and fully capable of doing what adults do. But no, that's not what's happening now. Hank has shut down. None of this adds up based on what she knows about him. This has stopped making any kind of sense to her.

Becky Rant can't imagine the expression she has on her face. It must be one of confusion, disbelief, and, if she's being honest, a little hurt. She runs through the evening in her head at lightning speed, picking at the details, the evidence, trying to find a clue as to what just happened.

There are none to be found.

This was not part of the plan.

She heard he went off the reservation after the job got to be too much, but this was not what she expected. Not at all. Seduction was a large part of her plan. She was so convinced that was the easy part that she didn't spend a second of her time thinking of an alternate plan. If she's being honest, somewhere between the jog and enchiladas things amped up and shifted from a line item on her plan to wanting to sleep with him for fun. Makes the seduction much easier in her experience. She needed seduction to lead to information. Sex to find honesty from him. It wasn't an elegant plan, not one guaranteed to be successful, but it was all she had.

She looks to him. There's something going on behind his eyes.

Almost like a wound that he's nursing.

Hank stands, keys out, his eyes already on the door. "You ready?"

"Yeah, guess I am."

1 YEAR AGO (LOS ANGELES)

Becky Rant and Johnny stand in front of a luxury condo building.

Necks craning, shielding their eyes from the California sun, both taking in the towering monument of glass, steel and new money. Their expressions are muted, at best. Neither one wrapped in the awe of the spectacle or troubled by the sore thumb of capitalism stuck in the middle of their old stomping ground.

The area has changed greatly over the years.

They used to run riot through these street with their hair on fire. Used to chase and be chased. Laughs, tears and blood shared between the three of them while weaving in and out of the blocks that surround this building.

That was years ago.

Now the area is a hipster haven, filled with over-priced coffee shops, craft beer bars and oddly specific clothing boutiques. The grime of crime has been wiped away, and a fresh coat of progress slapped on for good measure. Right or wrong, better or worse is not for them to judge. If they were being honest, Johnny and Becky Rant would tell one another how much better the streets look. But that would mean opening up the past and examining it for what it was. Not something that interests either one of them, not right now at least. This is a reunion of sorts.

"Crazy," Becky Rant says, looking around the old neighborhood.

Johnny nods.

She reaches over and holds his hand, wrapping her fingers in his. His much larger paw of a hand swallows hers as she squeezes as tight as she can. It's a comforting gesture they'd done over the years. Never meant anything more than *I'm here*. Something they've both done with Isabel as well. The three of them often held hands and shared hugs as often as possible without the need to define their affection or explain it to one another, or anyone else for that matter.

"Coffee?" she says, pointing to a place located at the ground floor of the building. "I'll buy."

"Sold."

They take a table by the window after their six dollar Guatemalan pour-overs are ready. The steam rolls from the large mugs plastered with a simple black and white logo. This is first time they've seen each other in a while.

Maybe years. Jesus, is that right? she thinks.

The three of them had gotten together on a fairly regular basis, but recently their lives have taken them in different directions. It's become harder and harder to find time. They text and email but it's not the same as being face to face in the same space. The times they've shared cannot be replicated. There's no way to have the same connection with another human being and they know it.

Life, unfortunately, has a way of dividing people over time.

Whether wanted or fought like hell, it happens to the best of them.

Johnny looks like he always did. Handsome. Big. Tough guy that carries himself like someone you'd want to avoid, but she and Isabel know there's a kindness to him that few will know. A kindness they will never take for granted. They sit enjoying the silence. Soaking up the joy of not having fill every moment with words. The brand of comfortable quiet that can only come from being around a select few in this life. They take a sip. They lock eyes, can't help but break into a laugh.

"Damn, hate to say it out loud, but damn that's good coffee," Johnny says.

"Yeah, hurts a little to like this so much."

"You look tired," Johnny says, leaning back, taking in the bags under red-streaked eyes.

"Nice to see you too, asshole."

"Sorry. You look great, but tired as hell."

"Better."

"What's going on?"

"Been working, man. Trying to earn."

Johnny nods. He wants to dig into it but stops. He's learned when to tap the brakes with Becky Rant and when to put the pedal down. This is a tap the brakes kind of day.

"How's that new gig going?" Becky Rant asks, wanting to move the conversation along. "Movie crap, right?"

"Yeah, working production around town. Some in Canada. I like it. Long, messed up hours, but I'm having a good time."

Becky Rant can't wipe the smile off her face. She knows how hard Johnny has worked to turn things around. Kick a few old bad habits. Habits that Becky Rant currently wears like a robe. She wants to ask him questions. Ask him how he's done it, pick his brain about where to begin, but that would take some form of advanced introspection that she does not possess at the moment. She can see the outer edges of pulling it together but she's not there. And she knows it.

"Kinda pissed at Isabel," Johnny says, running a thick finger around the lip of the oversized coffee mug.

"Why?"

"Really?" He puts his hands out. "She's not here."

"Oh, you mean growing and dropping children out of you doesn't buy her a rain check?"

"Priorities, Becky Rant. That's all I'm saying."

Becky Rant snickers, rolls her eyes, then takes a look around the place. Oddly, this is very familiar spot for both of them. She stomps her foot on the hardwood floor.

"You think they'd let us fight? For old times' sake?" She asks with a spark in her eyes.

"Doubtful."

"You know, we were here first. Before they put this damn building in."

"I can ask management for a ruling?" Johnny sips his damn good coffee. "You realize it's been about five things before this building?"

"Not the point."

"Hey," Johnny says, trying again, with his voice coated in concern. "You're okay, right?"

"Don't change the subject, dickhead. I'll beat your ass in the middle of this warm bean juice shop."

"Tell me you're okay."

"I'm fine."

He looks her over. She's starting to burn inside. He can see it.

"Really?" He presses anyway.

"Really." She sighs. "I'm fine. I'll get there, ya know."

Johnny nods, letting it go again.

"I think the three of us turned out pretty damn okay." She raises her coffee in a toast. "Considering the disasters we could have been."

Johnny considers the statement, then says, "True."

They touch cups. They share a smile. A giggle. A slice of quiet looks between them.

"Really miss beating your ass," Johnny says, looking out the window.

"Eat me," she says with a grin.

1 YEAR AGO (CARDIFF-BY-THE-SEA, CALIFORNIA)

Hank is in bed with a woman.

They are as passionate now as they were their first time. Riley is a beautiful woman. Her dark, raven-like hair spreads out across the white sheets as her neck arches. A moan leaves her lips, curling into a smile. The moonlight illuminates her face wrapped with ecstasy. Groans roll. Sounds of heavy breathing. Rain pours down in sheets. The thunder claps after the lightning crashes outside the lavish hotel room.

Riley's eyes close tight.

Her mouth opens wide.

A silent moan followed by a whisper as she digs her nails into his broad back. Her orgasms are long, rolling waves. At least they are with him. She pushes her head back deep into the pillow as the rush of pleasure runs its course. As if a surge of electricity has shot through her, starting at her head and exiting through her balled up toes. He finishes as if on cue.

She has no idea how he does that.

The timing of this man.

It blows the mind.

Hank rolls off her. They both stare up at the ceiling. A smile on her lips. A focused, distant gaze in his eyes. Their hard breathing can barely be heard above the storm raging outside the hotel. Clothes litter the floor. A half-empty bottle of red wine sits on the nightstand. It matches the completely empty one in the living room. Their bodies tingle, hovering ever so slightly above numb. She thinks of taking up smoking again, laughs. He looks to her, his face solemn but caring.

"Can't believe I have to leave," Riley says.

"Now?"

"He gets back tonight."

"Oh, forgot it was so soon." He gets up from the bed, heading to the bathroom. The condom needs to be removed. "Where's he flying in from again?"

"Well, he's connecting in Atlanta, but he was in London, maybe, then Prague."

Hank slips off the condom, dropping it into the trashcan. As he washes his hands, he looks to his black leather overnight bag. His mind clicks into place off of her words. *Atlanta, London and Prague.* It was the locations he was looking for. All of this, the last few weeks with her, was about obtaining those three city names. His eyes begin to fill as he thinks of what's next. His face flushes fast to hot. His hands begin to tremble as he dries them with a towel.

"Prague?" He leans his head back as he asks the question, but it sounds more like he's repeating the answer he was looking for. Checking her for clarity.

"Yeah, some business thing. He's been going back and forth. Pretty much around the time we met."

Hank stares at the bag, almost looking through it.

She's the mistress of a San Diego businessman. A married man with two children. Newborn twins, a boy and a girl. He set her up well in the small beach town Cardiff-by-the-Sea that's nestled between San Diego and Los Angeles.

"Thank God I met you." She laughs again. "Maybe it's the orgasms that's got me babbling like this, but that guy is an asshole. He's a bad guy, ya know? I mean he's been okay to me, money and stuff, but he doesn't talk to me like you. Doesn't look at me like you."

Hank steps into the room.

Riley eyes the shadowy outline of his body in the moonlit doorway. She does some quick sex arithmetic along with a mental and physical inventory to determine if she can go again. It may be a little soon. He's good but he's not Superman, not to mention she's not sure she's ready either. Then she remembers that her guy, the bad guy, is arriving soon. She bites her lip, realizing again that this is goodbye. At least for a little while.

"When will I see you again?" she asks, getting up on her elbows.

Hank says nothing.

"Sean? You okay?"

Hank likes to go with S names. Sean, Sam, Steve, Scott...

"Yeah," Hank says, fighting through his shaky voice.

Hank raises his gun and fires two silenced shots into Riley's head.

Hank enters the cheap highway diner.

The rusty bell on the door clinks, barely audible above the storm. He's drenched from the rain. His high-priced shirt and jeans cling to his muscular frame. His hair drips. Drops of rain run down his face. Staring toward the back of the place, he sees his guy.

His handler.

His limited connection to the Agency.

It's pretty empty this late on a Tuesday, only about an hour or so until closing. At a booth in the back, a man sits by the window. He's dressed in a dark suit slick from the rain. His short haircut is all but dry, with a few spots of rain drying on his forehead. He hasn't been here long. Not long enough to get completely dry. Hank knows this man chose the table by the window so he could see Hank come in. He chose a table at the back so Hank couldn't come up on him unnoticed. It's what Hank would have done.

The man glances toward Hank, takes a sip of his coffee, then looks back out the window, watching the rain dump down in buckets.

Hank slides in across from the man in the dark, wet suit.

"London, maybe, then Prague. Coming into San Diego through Atlanta."

"Prague?" Dark Suit asks. His eyes never leave the rain while digesting the information. Hank can see his brain churning, processing the angles.

"He's been going back and forth." As the words leave Hank's mouth his expression drains along with them. With a half-smile he waves off the waitress who attempts to pour him coffee. Can't look her in the face.

"You believe her? Is Hector's little sex toy reliable?"

Hank clenches his fist under the table. "I do."

"What's her damn name?"

"It was Riley."

"OK. So you think Riley's info is actionable?"

"Yeah, again, I do." Hank's anger spikes as the Man in the Dark Suit so casually discounts everything about her. "She had no reason to lie. Nothing to gain."

The Man in the Dark Suit considers this for a moment as he continues to watch the storm rage outside the window. He takes a deep breath, then lifts up and slides a black computer bag across the table.

"Nice job," he says, shooting a finger-gun toward Hank.

Hank locks eyes with him. He doesn't like this guy, never did, but those two words are digging into Hank's head like a drill. Something about the word *job* isn't sitting well with him. As he grips the strap of the computer bag, his hands begin to shake again.

The Dark Suit's eyes slip from Hank back to the world outside the window. "Get some rest. We'll clean the hotel room. Make it all go away." He turns to Hank with a nod. "We'll be in touch soon." The Man in the Dark Suit goes back to his coffee, goes back to his careful study of the rain.

Hank's face is void of expression.

His thousand-yard stare out into nothing.

He thinks about killing the Dark Suit right here in

the booth. Fantasizes about putting two into his skull and disappearing out into the night. Becoming a ghost. A reset button that could get pressed by simply pulling the trigger on this Man in the Dark Suit. It would be so easy to do. So right. So justified.

But he doesn't.

Hank pulls the bag over his shoulder and leaves the table without a word.

Walks out into the storm.

8 DAYS AGO (ROUGH CREEK, TEXAS)

Hank tips a long pour of whiskey into his coffee.

His eyes are heavy.

Sleep is a memory.

Hank hasn't thought about Riley and that rainy night in Cardiff-by-the-Sea in a long time.

Sipping his coffee, he stares out the window that overlooks the motel and the stretch of highway that cuts along the front. It's not heavy traffic by any measure, but there is a spattering of cars and trucks that buzz back and forth occasionally. An eighteen-wheeler roars by every so often, providing a desired change of pace. Ever since they upped the speed limit to seventy, this part of the highway seems to have a lot more life.

Again, not heavy traffic, but it's consistent, mornings

in particular. Mostly truckers and working stiffs with shit jobs and even shittier hours. Hank enjoys the sound. There's a rhythm to it that he enjoys. Dead silence, then the zip of a car followed by the slightly heavier sound of a rolling truck, then the roar of a rig. It's soothing. Hank's own private, soothing, country-ocean sounds.

Being on the highway helps with the motel biz, but Hank's clients are mostly teenagers and adultery enthusiasts. He knew this before he bought the place, but he didn't really understand. Now he understands. He used to clean the rooms himself. Found it therapeutic in a way, and him picking up the task saved a few bucks. But after high school graduation season, no more. Hank has seen a lot in his lifetime, but that was disgusting. He found a couple of nice local ladies about a week ago who were looking for a side hustle and didn't mind the occasional display of bodily fluid. Working the day to day of the motel has helped him forget.

He's made forgetting an art form.

Stuffing things away, pushing them under until there's only a hint of hurt that lingers. A dull ache of a memory, like after a heavy workout. His work with the Agency, his time in the Marines, he's all but erased that from the hard drives in his skull. There's a residue, a film, that remains however. It coats his body and mind and he can't wipe them clean no matter how hard he tries. Not completely at least. Random fragments remain and come back to him at unpredictable times.

This town helps.

This whiskey helps.

He pops a pill. Those help too. He's tried them all. He was surprised how quickly and easily he found access to the little helpers in this town. Within days, he had all the bottles he needed. That's how he knows about the side biz going on at the bar with Fossil Woman and her son. The pills scare him, but they are helpful. Handy in helping Hank shove it all aside and move on.

He's been able to remove himself from basic wants and needs. He keeps to himself. He drinks. He works on the motel rooms. He pops pills. He doesn't sleep, but hey, he's catching up on all the TV he's missed.

But then she showed up.

Becky Rant stumbled into his peaceful, self-directed amnesia and flipped a switch inside him.

She's smart and funny.

She's attractive.

He can't do this.

She needs to leave.

He pours more "juice" into his coffee. Needs to stop thinking about her. About how he turned down an evening with her. Even in Hank's experience, it's rare for a woman to come out and ask. There's a game of give and take. Hints and maybes. She removed all that and he, in turn, shut down. He couldn't do it.

Hank picks up his coffee and heads into the living room. He started reading the Roosevelt biography a few days ago. Great read. He thumbs through a few pages, but sets it back down. Can't hold onto a steady string of concentration. Sips his coffee. His mind unwinds, dissecting what he knows about her.

About Becky Rant.

He *jogged* around Fossil Woman's house, trying to keep an eye on her. Him running into her outside that house wasn't as fate-like as it appeared. His reasons were twofold. One, he didn't know what a woman like her was doing in a place like this, and two, he knows what Fossil Woman and her dumbass boy are involved in. Some dirty business they shouldn't be.

Yes, this Becky Rant is smart, funny, and easy on the eyes, but she also wants something. That much is clear. Something more than a playful spin in a motel room with a stranger in a small Texas town. He's been trained to charm and seduce, to create trust and project an overwhelming feeling of being wanted. Highly skilled at making someone feel like they are the most special person on the planet. It was his job. He was good at it.

She's good at it too.

Is she naturally gifted, or is she trained as well?

Probably a bit of both. Not trained in the traditional sense, like he was, more like she has been molded over time by the world of men. The eyes that have been on her during the course of her lifetime. The attention paid to her. Sometimes sought after and other times, perhaps most times, forced upon her by men she'd rather avoid. She didn't wake up one day looking like that. She's been a magnet for men her whole life, engineering her wit and defenses into a finely-tuned machine over the years. This much he knows. Part survival, part learning to use what you've got to get what you want.

Hank goes upstairs, taking his coffee along with him.

Things got blurry for Hank last night. He allowed himself to enjoy her company. It's impossible to turn off his skillset, but he did enjoy the time he spent with her yesterday. True enjoyment. The way they talked. The back and forth. The way she looked at him. Having an honest connection with a woman has been missing for some time.

It's a confusing thing for Hank. Confusing for him to try and understand when the art of manufactured seduction he's learned separates from a true attraction in the real world. Can they be separated from one another?

Perhaps not for him.

Probably not anymore.

When does the training drop off and honest feelings

creep in? When does the curated version of him fade away and the honest one take over? The version of Hank that dated girls in high school. Hank at homecoming. At keg parties, fumbling over bras in the woods. Hank slow dancing at prom. The version before he was recruited out of the Marines. When the Agency plucked him directly from the dogs of war and tossed him into the role of lady-killer.

What was I last night?

Honest Hank, or manipulative killer?

Is there a difference anymore?

From time to time he tries to remember their names. His assignments. He used to be able to, but now he can't even recall the name of the first one. Even her face is blurred in his memory. He's not sure whether he hates his brain for forgetting or is thankful for the defense it's providing him. Cardiff-by-the-Sea isn't the only place Hank remembers.

He remembers San Diego.

He enjoyed her company as well.

Isabel wasn't that long ago.

Hank walks down the long hallway. Its polished, original wood floor creaks under his bare feet. He loves this house. Its feel. The way it smells and wraps itself around him. The place is dark, yet warm and inviting all at once. Part of the place gives off the vibe of the home of a creepy old man who does unspeakable evil inside. A home where a diabolical professor is doing Frankenstein-like experiments at all hours of the night. Nothing even vaguely like that happens here, but like Hank, the house keeps people at arm's length.

The real estate agent made a joke that the kids think the place is haunted. She assured Hank it wasn't, thinking it might scare him off. It didn't; it was actually what sold him. It feels secure to him. It has become home to him in a short amount of time.

He sips his coffee then turns the knob to a room at the end of the hall. The room is tiny. A guestroom of sorts. A small single bed, a waist-high dresser, and a hand-knitted, made by grandma style blanket spread over a rocking chair in the corner. Hank opens the closet door. Inside are stacks of sheets, folded blankets, old magazines and a few random old towels. He carefully picks up and moves a specific pile of sheets that rests on the floor. Setting them on the bed, he turns back, staring at the space he's created in the closet.

His jaw sets.

A woman like Becky Rant doesn't wander into a town like this without a reason.

What's her reason? Her why?

What do I know about Becky Rant?

He could fill a thimble with what he knows about her.

Could fill a body bag with what he doesn't.

Behind the sheets is a black safe about the size of large microwave. Hank crouches down and punches in an eight-digit code. There's a green light, a beep, then the door clunks open. Inside are three handguns, all 9mm Glocks, two boxes of shells, a few magazines, and a steel tactical knife. There's also three stacks of hundred-dollar bills, along with a shorter stack of prepaid credit cards, two passports, and an old picture of his mother, the edges frayed and tattered.

Hank stands up. Sips his coffee.

What the hell does she want?

What is Becky Rant's why?

Stepping over to the window, he glances down at the motel.

Becky Rant lies awake in her motel bed.

The sun pokes through the blinds, cutting lines through the box-like room.

She reviews last night. Flips it over and over again in her mind. The way Hank withdrew. How quickly he retreated back into himself. It happened so fast, he went so cold so damn fast, she really didn't know what to do. Sure, seduction was part of the plan, a big part of her bigger plan, but after a beer, half a margarita, some eyes and his boyish charm, her plan of seduction became more about want than project necessity. She hates how weak she is sometimes. This is the type of thinking she has to undo.

She's needed now.

People are depending on her. Depending on her to not pop pills and not screw the lady-killer simply for giggles. Those people need her to be her best self. To finish the damn plan and keep her damn promise.

She's trying not to take it personally, but rejection is not something she's used to.

Not sure she likes it.

No, she's damn sure she doesn't like it.

Sitting up in bed, a rush of blood floods her head, hitting her like a wrecking ball. She didn't get snot-slinging drunk last night, but it was just enough to create a fog for the next day. She presses on the rising fire in her chest. Damn cheap enchiladas. As she gets up, she catches a look at herself in the tall mirror standing near the bathroom. The bruises on her body are dark, black with some hints of purple and blueish reds in her flesh. There are various, smaller hurt-shapes scattered on her arms and shoulders. A large one on her thigh, and a long scratch, more like a cut, across her stomach. She's used makeup to cover the more visible marks, but since she washed her face last night the bags under her eyes, along with the pop she took to her jaw and cheek, are showing this morning.

She thinks of Ronald Church. The look on his face when he thought he killed her.

Son of a bitch.

She clenches her fist and makes a muscle like a champ in the mirror, then laughs.

Seems like forever since she's seen the inside of a gym. Really it was only a few days ago. She's worked hard to stay in shape. Real hard lately. Lately she's had to prepare. Prepare for what happened a few nights ago on the beach with Ronald. In addition to the LAPD boxing sessions, she frequented a swank LA gym. She's been a bit of a workout warrior most of her life, so she started at a good baseline, but she really poured it on lately. The MILFs and would-be actresses had no idea they were sweating next to a dead woman.

Becky Rant worked those weights hard as hell to get to be dead.

Getting killed without being killed required strength. In more ways than one. The *light* days were her spin-yoga days, and those really helped her with flexibility and stamina. Both much needed in her big fight.

Her dramatic finish.

Her third act climax before dying.

Becky Rant limps over to the motel bed and throws on a T-shirt. She's tired of thinking about all that unpleasant crap.

Wounds out of sight, wounds out of mind.

Am I out of my mind? she wonders.

Her hands shake. She shakes them back hard, trying to break the cycle of trembling. Coming off the pills and the booze isn't going be easy. That much she knew already.

None of this is going to be easy, dummy.

She's slipped here and there with booze and pills, she knows it, but she's trying like hell. That man did this to her. Ronald kept her where he wanted her. Kept her drugged and in a suburban, docile state like a captive tiger in a petting zoo. He fed her lies along with the drugs. Made her believe it was all her choice and not his. Killing her when he was done with her was also his choice.

Faking her death was hers.

She knows she has to keep things tight or this plan will never work. And by not working, she means not living. She's realistic. There's a very good chance Ronald will find out she's alive, but every day he thinks she's dead the better. He's probably searching high and low right now. There was no body for them to find. They'll more than likely link the stolen BMW as well.

Her black duffle bag rests in the corner. Unzipping the bag, she takes a step back, giving it a long look. Given the fog she's under, she wants to be able to make a wide-angle assessment. A gun, two magazines, some zip ties, duct tape, a few razor blades, a cell phone, and three rubber band-bound stacks of cash in random bills. There's also a bottle or two of pills, along with a couple of airplane bottles of Dewar's next to a strip of condoms.

Everything a girl needs for a night out on the town. She smirks to herself.

Damn she wishes she had some coffee.

She eyes the Dewar's and the pills. Every molecule of her being wants to grab them both and drain their contents into her mouth like a baby bird being fed by mama.

But she doesn't.

She still wants the coffee, however.

The phone inside the bag buzzes. It's a prepaid burner she picked up a few days ago. Only one person has the number. Becky Rant jumps to pick it up.

"Everything okay?" she asks.

"Yes," a kindly-sounding older woman says. "I just wanted—"

"Are they okay? What's wrong?"

"Everything is fine. I just wanted to check in and tell you everything is fine."

"Thank you." Becky Rant breathes out, letting her sudden anxiety spike settle down. "I'm sorry. It should only be a few more days." Her eyes slip over to her bag. The anxiety spike returns, rising higher this time. "I hope, at least."

"Okay, that sounds good. We're doing just fine. I'll check in later," the kindly old woman says, then hangs up.

Dropping the phone on the bed, Becky Rant's mind churns cement mixer style. Her eyes fade in and out as she stares at the contents of her open bag. Her heart starts to return to a normal pattern. As much as the call scared the hell out of her, she's thankful for it. That call was a much-needed reminder about what is important. About what this plan is all about. She goes back to taking inventory of the bag. Something is off. Something's missing.

Her face drops.

Her brain ignites.

She touches her neck. The half-heart on the chain is gone.

How did I miss it?

She noticed it was missing when she bolted from Fossil Woman's house, but she was distracted. Knocked off course by Hank. Never returning to the thought, she didn't close the loop and work the problem through to a conclusion. Her anger spikes. Mad at herself. She can't do this. Can't make these kind of mistakes if she's going pull off her promise. The people she's up against don't make mistakes.

How am I going to do this if I can't keep up with a damn necklace?

Digging through the bag, her hands move fast, shoving its contents aside left and right in a search that's growing in intensity by the second. She doesn't remember taking the chain off. She'd never take it off. Not something so damn important to her. Something that cannot be replaced. The only thing she has left in the world that's hers.

When she safely left the scene of her death, she put it back around her neck, not to be removed until it was time. It's something she's going to give to them when the time is right. She moves fast over to the jeans lumped on the floor from last night. Digging through the pockets, she comes up empty.

She paces as her mind sets fire.

"Shit."

Running her fingers through her hair, the anger-tears begin to form, swelling in the corners of her eyes, dying to drop down her face. Her hands begin to shake again, but for a different reason now.

Think. Think. Think. Where is it?

Wearing nothing but a T-shirt, underwear and her bruises, she bolts out from the door, rambling headlong toward the BMW. She doesn't care. She's becoming more and more frantic as she plows through the car checking the glovebox, the center console, the trunk —nothing.

"Shit. Shit. Shit."

She reviews her timeline. Where has she been? She retraces her steps. Last night. Her dinner with Hank. Jogging with Hank. What else? Think.

"Shit."

She retraces her steps. The bar. Her unwanted stay at Fossil Woman's house.

She closes her eyes and exhales. "Shit." In all the crazy she forgot.

"You okay?"

Becky Rant spins, finding Hank standing behind her holding two cups of coffee.

He offers one to her.

"I need to go to that damn bar," she says, grabbing the cup.

PART TWO

"Shame," Robot Woman's voice crackles.

Becky Rant sits straight up. She'd been talking, telling her story, for so long she almost forgot there was someone on the other end of the conversation. Folding her hands over each other, she locks her fingers together while staring at the black speaker waiting for more. More words to help connect the dots.

She gets nothing.

Gives it a minute or two.

"Shame what? What's a shame? Or are you saying shame on me?" she asks, an eye roll in her voice.

"It's a shame he wouldn't sleep with you."

Becky Rant's ears perk up. This is new.

"It was unfortunate," she says.

"I never heard of anyone passing up the great Becky Rant."

This is about as close to a conversational tone Becky Rant has heard since she's been in here. That was a slip. A crack in the wall. Is Robot Woman loosening up, or screwing up?

This woman knows quite a bit about me.

She just said it. She's heard about me.

There was something oddly personal about what she just said. The words she chose. Hinting that Becky Rant was someone men wanted. Suggesting she's been told some stories about the *great Becky Rant*. Stories about men, maybe from men. Meaning Robot Woman is possibly annoyed by the stories. Tired of hearing about the *great Becky Rant*. Jealous, perhaps.

The list of potential captors is still at two, but now leaning strongly toward one.

She attempts to draw Robot Women out even farther. "Happens to the best of us, right?"

There's a pause. A crackle, then, "Not what I was told. Not with you."

"Gotta admit, it stung a little."

"I bet."

Becky Rant tries to hide her excitement. She's bouncing inside. She can't believe the sudden shift in Robot Woman's conversational pattern. She had been guarded. Distant. Exhibiting no traits that even slightly resembled a human being. Offering up only short phrases, if any, and minimal contact. There was the bit about the pills, but now she's downright chatty. Little bitchy, but whatever, she has opened the gates. Hearing the sound of a woman's voice threw her at first, but now she's almost one hundred percent sure who's thrown her into this box.

Still, this Robot Woman is puzzling.

Why the whiplash-fast change in her tone and mood? What triggered this conversational good fortune? Then the pieces snap together in Becky Rant's head.

Robot Woman has been left alone.

There's been someone holding a leash on her all this time, and now she's by herself. Nobody there to push *mute* like they did earlier. Maybe they coached her before, but had to do it in a hurry. Maybe she didn't want to do any of this and is doing this Robot bit against her will.

This attitude of hers has always been there, slightly below the surface, but there nonetheless. It's just whoever was in that room with her before is now gone. Why she's been left alone is a whole other question, but Becky Rant can only deal with one thing at a time. Right now, it's just her and Robot Woman, and Robot Woman has some things to say. It's up to Becky Rant to keep it rolling.

She leans in closer to the speaker, adds some vulnerability to her voice. "That ever happen to you?"

Silence.

Becky Rant starts again. "Now, I wouldn't call it straight-up rejection—"

"Really?"

"No," Becky Rant presses, "but I suppose that's what it was, if I'm being honest. You ever have that?"

A crackle, then nothing. This *nothing* is Robot Woman not speaking, rather than being silenced by someone else. That's a win in Becky Rant's book. Robot Woman digesting the question instead of her voice being policed. A big damn difference.

"Come on, now," Becky Rant offers with a smile. "Don't shut down on me. I bet it's never happened to a woman like you. Not with that hot as hell sex-bot thing you've got going. You start in with the dirty robot talk, toss around that filthy AI mouth, I bet the pants drop and the dicks dance like prom night."

"I do fine."

"I'm sure you do. Tell me about it."

"I have plenty of sex. Too much, actually."

"Don't doubt it. Give me details. It's just us girls, right?"

"Stop."

"I'm bored as hell in here, gorgeous. Lay down some speaker-sex stories for me."

"You're crazy." There's what sounds like a robotic snicker. "I'm not—"

"You said you do fine. Who are you doing?"

"You know who."

Becky Rant struggles to keep her eyes from popping from her head. In the back of her mind she knew, but it was just confirmed. The intensity in her face fades. The fire behind her eyes dies off as the realization washes over her.

Ronald Church is holding her here.

In a way, she's relieved. Thankful it's not Hector and Isabel's people. It makes sense. Those people would just gut her and not bother with questions. Her shoulders slump. She also now knows that Robot Woman is with Ronald in some way. A wave of sadness washes over Becky Rant. Not from knowing Ronald is with someone new, not that at all, but sadness for what he's probably done to this new woman.

I have to help.

Somehow.

"Did he..." Becky Rant turns, looks toward the dark glass, hopefully looking at the woman behind the glass.

Imagines eye contact with Robot Woman. "What did he do to you?"

A long pause.

Speaker crackles, then Robot Woman says, "Nothing."

"Right." Becky Rant nods. "Nothing, nothing at all."

"He's a good man."

Becky Rant explodes up from her chair. "He's a piece of shit."

"He tries. He cares so much. He's getting better."

"That why I'm here? The last few days have been about, what? His path to *better*?"

"Stop."

"Cut me loose. Let me go."

"No."

"Help me out of here. I can help you."

"I don't need your goddamn help," Robot Woman barks. Her electronic-coated words echo, fading off into a renewed silence. It's as if the temperature in the room went from a hundred degrees to negative ten with a simple snap of her fingers.

Becky Rant stops. Resets.

She's hit a nerve, needs to pull back or risk losing Robot Woman forever.

"Sorry. Of course you don't need my help, or anybody else's. Didn't mean it that way." Becky Rant holds the speaker in her hands like a delicate egg. As if holding a loved one's face. "But we can help each other, right? I can't do a damn thing chained up like an animal. We, *we*, can do something. We can fix this. I know you want him gone. All you gotta do is— "

The sound of a door opening comes from the speaker.

A quick shuffle of feet.

"No," Becky Rant whispers.

The door slams.

There's the sound of a chair pushing back, scraping against the floor. Becky Rant felt a slight tremor in the walls when the door slammed. A vibration in the floor when the chair scraped. It confirms that *they* are, without a doubt now, behind that dark glass.

Hard whispers bark through the speaker.

Becky Rant presses her ear close to the speaker, trying to catch at least a single word of what feels like an argument in there. Robot Woman is in trouble, she's guessing. She's pretty sure she makes out at least three different voices. It's hard because they all sound like robots through whatever voice modifier they're running. At least two of them are male.

There's a sudden, halting silence.

Damn mute button has been pressed.

Becky Rant slams the speaker back down on the

table. Stares at the glass. Breathes in deep, in and out, fighting to find some sense of calm inside of her. Waits. Struggles, searches to find that part of her that doesn't want to break and burn. Prays that everything that just happened, her conversation with Robot Woman, wasn't a complete waste of time. Hopes that the crack in the wall Robot Woman opened up isn't now sealed. Silenced forever. Becky Rant hopes she isn't a reason for her getting hurt. A reason for her to be punished. Ronald Church can get real creative when he puts his mind to it.

"It's not her fault," Becky Rant says to whoever is listening.

She gets as close to the dark glass as the chain will allow. The steel cuff cuts into her ankle as she strains for every centimeter. Becky Rant wants them to see her face. Wants her message to be heard loud and clear.

"Hey!" she yells, pointing her finger at the glass. She sees only herself, but she knows who's back there. "Your problem is with me, not her."

Becky Rant feels her teeth grind.

Every muscle in her body is pulled tight to the point of stone.

The speaker crackles.

"Tell us a story," Robot Woman says.

8 DAYS AGO (ROUGH CREEK, TEXAS)

"I lost something," Becky Rant says, white-knuckle gripping the wheel.

"Okay," Hank says. His fingers dig into the dashboard, struggling to find a feeling of safety. His new friend is driving like a crazy person. "What? What did you lose?"

Becky Rant cuts the wheel hard. Jams the pedal down. Hank jerks to the right, almost slamming his face on the passenger window. Becky flips off an eighteen-wheeler, then lays on the horn.

"It has to be at the bar." She talks while working it out as the words exit her mouth. "At least that's where we'll start."

"What are you talking about?"

"A necklace." She hates that she has to explain this

to him. It's too soon. Sooner than she wanted, but she's fresh out of choices at the moment. She'll recalibrate, reset, and alter the plan later. "It's a silly gift between me and a friend. I had it on a chain. I can't find it."

"And you're sure it's at the bar?"

"I'm not sure of a damn thing. If it's not there, then we might have to go strong at that whacko's house, but—"

"I'm sorry. *Go strong at that whacko's house?*"

"BUT... I do know that I don't have it now and I did have it while driving to this dump. Jesus, this may be the first city modeled after a donkey's butthole." She looks to Hank. She realizes she needs to bring it in and not insult the town. The man does live here. "Sorry, this is a nice town. I'm just a little pissed off over here."

"I get it. Let's not go in with our hair completely on fire, okay? It's like ten in the morning."

"Oh no. Are they open?"

"Well, of course, it is a weekday. Marlin and Andy start up with the drink around eight thirty, then Carol drops off her kids and rolls in around nine or so."

Becky Rant slow turns toward him.

He shrugs. No apologies. He's got problems too.

She toys with the idea of asking why he knows this, but decides that's another conversation for another time. She's heard he might be on the bottle more than he should. She counted on it when piecing together the plan. Broken is easier to work with.

The BMW skids to a stop in the gravel in front of Rattle Battle Bar.

Hank scrunches his nose. This is not what he expected. Becky Rant takes note of his expression, then looks toward the parking lot. There's a long line of motorcycles parked along the front row. She looks to Hank. His eyes are on the line of choppers and hogs. It's as if he's calculating, working through a lengthy word problem. She can tell this is new. Something he either hasn't seen before, or he's seen it before and doesn't like it.

"Not the regulars, Hank?" she asks.

"How bad do you want this thing of yours?" he asks without looking her way.

"Real bad, Hank."

"Like I said, there's been talk about the dumbass son running some things out of the bar. On the side. I've never asked much about it. Never really wanted to get involved."

She opens the door, not requiring more explanation. "Well, Hank, I'm about to get heavily involved."

Doesn't matter to her who's in there. She'll chop down the devil himself if she has to. This is the Rant part of her name. Blinded by what she needs to do, caution is not in her vocabulary. She's got one foot out of the car as she stab-presses the trunk release. Rounding the bumper, she reaches the opening trunk, digs in and pulls something out from under a blanket.

Hank steps out from the car. Cool and calm, but more than a little puzzled.

Becky Rant storms toward the bar with a rubber-gripped hammer held tight in her fist, letting it sway by her side. She likes hammers. Loves them, actually. Easy to get, they're light, swing fast like a fist, and crush like a dream.

Hank steps back, glancing into the open trunk. Inside, scattered among the spare tire, empty beer cans and next to her bag is a sawed-off 12-guage shotgun along with a few boxes of shells and a large butcher knife. Not normal packing for a getaway weekend. Hank's suspicions are confirmed. He's rarely wrong about these things, but her *why* is still a mystery.

A bell gives a dull-sounding ding.

Hank looks up.

Becky Rant plows through the door of the Rattle Battle.

Hank stares, thoughts grinding behind his eyes. He blinks. He shuts the trunk then moves toward the front door of the bar. As he gets closer to the entrance he can hear the yelling, the screaming, the sporadic bursts of profanity before he even opens the door.

He balls his fists tight.

Takes a deep breath.

Stepping inside, Hank sees Becky Rant standing above a large man who's laid out on the floor with a wound between his eyes. A perfect bloody circle has taken up residence above his nose, centered between his bushy brows. Blood is seeping down the bridge of his nose, making a slow crawl into his eyes. He's not moving. He's out cold.

Hank watches.

Thinking.

Analyzing.

She swings the hammer, landing a crushing blow to another large biker's head, dropping him to his knees, then kicks him in the throat, sending him flying backward to the floor. The remaining three bikers step back, creating a half circle in front of her. They bark hard words at her like *bitch* and *whore*. Becky Rant takes a swing like Thor, missing one of them by a hair.

He's enjoyed his stay in Rough Creek, but Hank knows he'll have to relocate again. Not the first time. He did a similar move a few short months ago, after San Diego.

After Isabel.

Wiry Stick Boy trembles behind the bar. His anxiety started at his toes and has wormed its way up to his shaking face. Standing behind the relative safety of the bar, he holds a baseball bat, but doesn't seem like he's got a clue what to do with it. His mother put it there, and has only used it a few times. He never considered he'd ever need it.

"Who's fucking next?" Becky Rant screams. Veins pulse and thump along her neck. Her grip on the hammer is so tight her knuckles flash the look of bones. "All I want is what belongs to me."

Hank stands in the doorway a few feet back from her. He keeps his feet in position: one foot forward, one back at an angle. Perfect stance if he needs to shift his bodyweight or move forward fast. At the ready if he needs to get involved. His eyes shift between the two bikers on the floor and the three standing upright. Always watching their eyes and hands. He keeps his breathing smooth, controlled. Wants his heartrate steady. He offers the people in this room nothing with his expression. He wants to create a hole in the universe and sit, waiting for his time. If you looked at him, you'd be hard pressed to tell the difference between him watching a cooking show or Becky Rant beating the hell out of bikers with a hammer.

"You." She points her hammer at Wiry Stick Boy. "Get over here."

He shakes head.

"Come. Here."

She slams the hammer on the bar like a tomahawk. The hammer gets stuck in the wood and one of the bikers makes a move on her. Becky Rant spins, planting a foot into his balls, then jams a knee to his chin.

Hank inches closer, so slowly that no one notices.

In a single motion, she yanks her weapon free from the bar, swinging herself around, pointing her war hammer at the other remaining bikers. They've moved in closer, cutting the distance around her, but now freeze, their feet suddenly planted to the floor.

"Don't," she barks at them. She turns back to Wiry Stick Boy. "I lost something here the other night and you're going to give it to me."

"What?" Wiry Stick Boy stammers. "I don't—"

"A necklace. A small silver pendant on a chain. I need it."

"Don't know nothing about no damn necklace, you whacko bitch," Wiry Stick Boy spits out from his thin lips. Tough words, but he's shaky as hell.

Becky Rant squints, zeroes in on his scrawny neck.

"Is it..." She cocks her head. "Is it around your neck, you stupid asshole?"

Around his neck is a small, silver half-heart hanging down on a thin rope chain. He looks away, almost ashamed that he forgot it was hanging out there in the open.

She was wrong about one thing. She didn't lose it at the bar. He took it off of her while she was sleeping on his mama's couch. He liked watching her chest rise and fall and the glimmer of the silver was distracting. He's not too bright, but he's smart enough to leave that detail out of this conversation.

"Give me that necklace"—Becky Rant leans her body over the bar, gently tapping her bloody hammer to his forehead like a soft knock at a door—"or I'm going to slam this into your very limited brain over and over."

Feet shuffle behind her.

She whips her head around.

The two massive bikers have closed the open space between them. They are only about a foot away from her. Hank explodes between them like a flicker of light-ning fired from the sky. His fists move too fast to register. His hands grab, twist and punch, leaving the room with only the echo of bones cracking and massive slabs of biker bodies dropping.

It was over before it started.

Slick, smooth, effortless badass.

All five bikers are now on the dirty floor groaning in

pain, sucking in deep breaths through clenched teeth as crimson spiderwebs flicker from their lips as they wail. Small sprays of blood mixed with drops of spit and sweat pepper their faces.

"We should leave," Hank says, thumbing toward the door.

Becky Rant nods, turning back to Wiry Stick Boy. He might be pissing himself. She raises her hammer as if she's about to flatten the final nail. He removes the chain, then shoves it toward her without a hint of conversation. She smiles while grabbing him by the hair. Looks him in the eye before slamming his face on the hardwood bar with a crunch. His head whips back hard. His boney frame flops down behind the bar out of sight.

The door gives its dull ding. Hank holds the door open, waiting for her.

She puts the chain around her neck, then picks up her hammer.

Outside, they move quickly to the BMW. Hanks eyes scan the area constantly, looking to see who, if anyone, is watching, then he steps toward the driver's side. He knows the Rattle Battle doesn't keep cameras on the parking lot. He also knows the idiot son is at least smart enough to shut down the inside security cameras while he's doing his dirty deeds with the regional biker boys. They've got some time before anyone finds that scene in there, but they don't have forever.

"Let me drive," Hank says.

She tosses him a look.

"Please." His jaw sets.

She doesn't argue, slipping into the passenger seat. Laying the bloody hammer down on the floorboard, she gives her hands a hard shake. She lost feeling in them somewhere during all the unpleasantness in the bar. More than likely a combination of the impact from the hammer strikes (the vibrations are hard to get used to) and the adrenaline spiking hard as she took on men two times her size. She's done it before, but that too is something you never truly get used to.

"Is this your car?" Hank asks, cutting the wheel, shifting, then jamming the gas. He's driving with purpose but watching his speed. "Is this in your name?"

"No."

He nods. He assumed she lifted the car, but needed to ask the question all the same.

They ride in silence during the remainder of the short trip. Becky Rant is thankful for the quiet. She knows there will be questions, lots of them, some from him, some from her, but she'd rather not get into it right now. There will be a lot to discuss between them, but she just can't right now. It felt good to unleash. To plow a hammer into some heads. An unexpected release of all that has been bottled up over the last few days. She almost feels guilty for feeling so good right now.

Almost.

Hank drives the BMW up into the garage of his house on the hill above the motel. Turning to her, he speaks clear and direct. A different tone than she's heard from him. A different look in his eyes. Focus. Strength. A *playtime is over* vibe that she oddly appreciates. These aren't orders he's about to give, but they are not suggestions either. He is merely stating what needs to be done.

"Get what you need from the trunk. Find another car, something plain, unremarkable, grab your things from your room and meet me in the parking lot outside your room." He pops the trunk.

Becky Rant understands, affirms with a nod, grabs her hammer, then heads toward the back of the BMW. Hank heads into the house without looking back at her. He still doesn't know her *why,* but he knows whatever it is, she's committed to it and she wants his help. Needs his help, is more like it. Even if she will never ask for it.

He sets a timer on his watch.

When he moved into the house, he practiced a drill, an exit strategy, though he truly hoped he wouldn't ever need to use it. His best time is under a minute. He's sure he can beat it, even under duress.

Becky Rant unzips the bag, shoving in the hammer, the twelve-gauge, and the shells. She leaves the butcher knife. No room. Besides, she knows she has a small tactical blade back in her motel room she usually keeps strapped to her ankle. During the rush this morning she had to leave it behind.

In her mind, she works through a quick checklist.

Her mental *to-dos*.

She wishes she had that dumbass pad with the peach and crap on it.

This is a change. A modification to her plan, but she always knew this would be a fluid situation. A living document. No time to recalibrate. She'll do that later. Right now she needs a new ride and to get everything out of that motel room. She'll need some time to wipe the room down. Get the sheets out of there. She can't leave anything a lab can use to identify her with later. The people looking for her, and there are several, are fairly skilled at that sort of thing, and she'll have a hard time explaining not being dead.

Snapping her fingers, she remembers she needs to wipe down the car as she throws the bag over her shoulder. She slams the trunk down with her elbow, then wipes it down with the bottom of her T-shirt. Setting down the bag on the trunk, she pulls out a pack of microfiber cloths she picked up just for this sort of thing. She wipes down the door handles, then the steering wheel, then everything she can remember touching. Even wipes over the areas she thinks she might have touched but isn't sure.

Gathering her things, she heads out of the garage.

"Need a ride," she says to herself, envisioning a check mark in a peach-colored box.

Feels bad about it, but she remembers seeing a few cars in a church parking lot down the street. A new ride is only a short jog away.

Hank moves like someone checking off a list as well.

There's a box of corn flakes inside the cabinet behind the coffee and a box of saltines. Digging inside, he lets the flakes spill out onto the counter as he digs out a small .38 in a plastic bag, then digs more, finding a roll of twenties. He pockets the twenties and slips the .38 in the small of his back.

Moving up the stairs, taking them two at a time, he hits the master bedroom. The place is immaculate. Not the room of a bachelor. No piles of dirty clothes. No buffet of odds and ends scattered across the dresser. His bed made tight enough to bounce quarters off of it.

In a hurry but not frantic, he enters the closet and pulls out a small bag. Very similar to the one Becky Rant has. Different color, his is dark blue, but the same brand. Unzipping it, he checks the kit that's packed with basic toiletries, neatly folded pairs of underwear, socks, two pairs of jeans, several black T-shirts along with a couple of blue ones, and one neatly folded dress shirt. There's also a Berretta, magazines and another roll of twenties.

Throwing the bag over his shoulder, he moves toward the guest room. The sheets he moved from the bottom of the closet earlier today are still stacked on the bed. Hank crouches down and punches in the eight-digit code. Hank removes the Glocks, the shells, the magazines, and a steel tactical knife, stuffing them into his bag along with the stacks of hundreds, the prepaid credit cards, two passports and the picture of his mother.

Scanning the bag, but not too long, he makes a quick inventory.

He's run through this scenario in his head many times.

He didn't know what would send him running from this house, from this town. Away from this new life. And he didn't think it would be this soon. Certainly didn't think it would be because of someone like Becky Rant.

But he knew this day would come eventually. He has a past. The kind of past that doesn't give up. This is why he knows how long it would take him to be packed up and on the run.

His watch beeps.

Upset he didn't beat his best time, Hank zips up the bag then tosses it over his shoulder. Another box checked for Hank. Reaching down to his wrist, he resets the timer on his watch to a new countdown, then heads down the stairs. He moves outside through the side door into the back yard. There's a small metal shed with a padlocked door near the house, but not too close. It stands toward the back of the yard near a tall fence.

He's reached part two of his exit strategy.

The '96 Ford F-150 skids to a stop in the dirt and rocks in front of the motel.

Becky Rant flies from the truck, heading toward her room. There's not much there to pick up. Most things are already packed in an identical black bag that was in the BMW trunk. If she were thinking better, she'd have the bags be different. She guesses it doesn't matter. She shoves the scattered clothes into the black bag, covering her gun, the rubber band-bound stacks of cash, and her other odds and ends with the clothes she wore yesterday. The pills, along with the airplane bottles of Dewar's and the condoms, are pushed to the edges of the bag, poking out the sides, making it look like a boa constrictor that's swallowed a small family of mice. Thankfully, there are only a few things in the bathroom that need to be packed up.

Every move has a purpose.

Every breath has meaning.

Zipping up the bag, she rushes out from the room. She tosses the bag into the floorboard of the truck then snatches up the microfiber cloths. Wipes down the door handles, the faucets in the sink, the toilet flusher, the TV remote, the TV—

"Don't need to do that," Hank says.

Becky Rant wipes away the sweat from her forehead with her arm.

"What? Why?"

"Like the truck."

"Do you?"

"I do." He motions to the door. "We need to go. Now."

Her eyes widen as she watches Hank pick up a container full of what smells like gasoline. He begins pouring it, making sure to spread it evenly around the bed, floor and walls. She steps out from the door, moves near the truck. There's a crackling sound. A whiff of smoke. A flicker of light coming from the house on the hill.

Hank's house is in the early stages of evolving into a full-on bonfire.

NOW

Becky Rant smiles at the dark glass, at herself in the reflection, then turns back to the black speaker resting on the steel table.

Its red light is shining, giving her a sign of life on the other end.

"Gotta tell ya, when he lit that little shitbox on fire..." Her eyebrows bounce with glee. "It did a little something for me."

"Okay," Robot Woman says.

"Thought I was going to have to switch out my panties. Know what I'm saying?"

"Yeah, we got it."

Becky Rant pats the table, then leans in.

"You just say *we?*"

White noise silence.

"Pretty sure I just heard *we*."

The *we* isn't a shock at this point. She's heard the hushed multiple voices on the other end. Becky Rant has known from the second she got here there was more than just Robot Woman. It's more the fact that Robot Woman just said it out loud. This is the second slip-up from her. She's not polished. Not used to this sort of thing. Not a pro at all. She's something else.

"Like to talk some more about my wet panties?"

"Stop," Robot Woman finally says.

Becky Rant leans back in her chair. Smiles big as hell. This is the most fun she's had since she got here. She doubles down.

"It's impressive what he did, right? Smoked his house, not to mention his business, without a moment of pause. Most women would run like hell after that. Me?" Clucks her tongue. "I've never wanted to have sex with someone so bad in my life."

"You always enjoyed a challenge," Robot Woman says.

Becky Rant nods.

Clucks her tongue again.

2 MONTHS AGO (SAN DIEGO, CALIFORNIA)

Isabel's pleasure groans fill the space of the large hotel suite.

The night air blows off the ocean, rippling the curtains.

Sweat beads across her perfect coffee-colored skin. Her dark hair falls inches from Hank's face as she braces her shaking body by holding on tight to his shoulders. After a moment of silent recovery, she pulls back while resting on top of him. Leaning back her head, she watches the shadows change shapes on the ceiling as her breathing returns to normal. Her eyes flicker. Her smile is wide.

Hank can't help but be drawn in by her.

She's a beautiful woman, that can't be argued, but that's not the only thing about her. Who she is and what she's built is nothing short of remarkable. Despite where you may sit on the great moral debate, right and wrong of drugs, legal or no, one has to marvel at what she's been able to accomplish.

Hank has spent the last several weeks getting to know her. They've spent a lot of time together, especially over the last few days. He was placed in the right place at the right time to meet her sixty-two days ago, but it was only recently that she truly let him into her life. Or as much as she was willing to. He knew she was lonely, had the files compiled by those who had watched her. It's lonely in her line of work. Hard to trust people in her world. The people she trusted put him in front of her.

He hates that she trusts him.

Hates the glowing, warm look in her eyes as she smiles down at him.

Hates what he has to do.

Isabel runs a finger down his chest, blowing Hank a kiss before slipping off of him. She giggles like a school-girl as she bounces toward to the bathroom, shutting the door behind her.

Hank lies in the bed.

Her perfume hangs in the air. He can still feel her. The touch of her skin, her breath on his neck. The smiles, the eyes, the way she looks at him burns holes into his mind. Her voice rattles around inside of his ears. Flash moments of pleasure-filled memories streak across his brain. Reaching for a half-empty bottle of wine, he sits up in bed drinking straight from the bottle. She wanted to meet at this high-end hotel this time.

A first for them.

Usually they would meet up at an out-of-the-way house near Laguna. A gorgeous, small home she called her *secret place*. At times, it felt like they were the only two people in the world when they were there. Hank worked hard to keep that place a secret. Kept it from the Agency too, even though the Man in the Dark Suit pressed him from time to time. Hank enjoyed the seclusion as much as she did. It was something for Hank to have for himself.

He can hear her singing from the bathroom.

They need this one to be messy.

That's what the Agency said.

Hank gets up from the bed, pulls on his T-shirt and jeans from the floor.

Want this one to look like a lover's spat gone wrong.

Hank pulls a tactical knife from his pocket. Flipping the blade open, he inspects the edge. Even in the darkness of the room, it finds some light. Small and sharp, and capable of great damage. Capable of a great *mess* in the right hands. Looking toward the bathroom door, he still hears the sweet sound of her singing. It pounds away at him like a pipe slamming over and over into the side of his head.

He knows the song.

It's a song she sings to her children when they cannot sleep. She told him about her kids. She has two. Boy and a girl a little over a year old. She hinted that raising them alone has been tough at times. Never a complaint, she's not the type to complain, but he could tell it has taken a toll on her. She worries about them. About them growing up without a father and not having any form of decent male role model. Her husband died a little over a year ago. Her Hector was killed, to be more precise, while returning from a business trip in Prague.

She's taken one lover since then.

She thinks his name is Stephen.

He knows his name is Hank.

It was the right time for them to meet. The intel gathered suggested that she was ready to move on. She was being more and more engaged with friends. Mentioned to an informant that she was getting back to normal. She joked with this same informant about how cute a waiter was. Before then, she'd never mentioned anything about men, let alone being attracted to one. She hired a private trainer and a nutritionist.

"She's getting her life back together after falling

apart," is what they told Hank when he started this assignment.

He can't imagine the woman he's gotten to know ever *not* having it together. Isabel's version of falling apart is probably more impressive than most *together* human beings on their best day.

Hank breathes in deep.

Last night, he mapped something out in his mind while working his way through a long pour of whiskey. He was staying at a much cheaper place a few miles from here. A motel off the freeway that took cash and didn't ask a lot of questions. As the whiskey worked the good burn, he decided how this would happen. She would go into the bathroom after sex as she always does. She hates the term *making love*. Sounds stupid to her. How do you *make* love? She enjoys more playful, fun terms. A smile with a flash of her eyes and she'd simply say, "Sex?" or "Let's go play." Sometimes it would be more direct, primal, no words at all. The more honesty the better for her. Her relentless honesty is what Hank likes most about her.

His eyes water.

His hand holding the blade trembles.

He reminds himself what her business does. It makes it easier for him. He thinks about what her people have done. She inherited Hector Blanco's violent industry, but she has talked about trying to change it. At first, she told him that she would do nothing to curb the violent practices started by her late husband, nor did she want to do anything to stop them for that matter.

Quite the opposite, in fact.

She wanted to grow it. Accelerate the ruthlessness. The files said she needed to send a message to the male-dominated business that a woman can sit in the big chair, that weakness is not the new policy. The message was clear. Isabel was running the show and her vagina wasn't going to be an issue. Hank's seen her work.

The photos of the dead.

The bodies.

The blood.

It's starting to wear her down though. Now, the violence isn't something she wants to continue. Isabel is having a change of heart. "I want it to stop," she said. She wants to shift the business, to stop all the senseless killing and use the enormous amount of cash they had amassed over the years to move the business in a new direction. Venture capital. Invest in local infrastructure around the globe. Make money while making a difference. She talked of how all the ugliness created by her husband's work can still do something worthwhile. She knew it wouldn't be easy.

Hank doesn't know if she's serious or not.

He doesn't have the luxury of believing her.

Trying to reconcile the woman he's gotten to know and the woman in the files has been a struggle for Hank. It's the hardest part of his job. She had a tough childhood. In and out of foster care in LA. All of his assignments had committed crime of varying degrees. Some had done horrible things. Some were threats to innocent people. Some were associated with monsters, and that, by proxy, made them monsters in the eyes of some.

One would think it gets easier each time.

It does not.

At least not for Hank. Each one of the women he's been assigned to kill stays with him. Some more than others, but they all take up residence in his heavy mind and hard heart.

Isabel is going to stay with him a long, long time.

He grips the knife tighter, eyeing the door.

He hasn't thought about the woman in Cardiff-by-the-Sea until now. He didn't spend much time with her, and if he's being honest, he didn't care about her the way he did some of the others. The fact that he can rank them by emotional attachment cuts into him more than he'd care to mention. Her name escapes him at the moment. Started with an R, maybe. Matter of fact, at this particular moment he's having a hard time remembering any of their names. He remembers a lot about them however.

He remembers he shot the woman in Cardiff-by-the-Sea a little less than a year ago.

She was very pretty. Lived the life of a kept beach girl. A fully paid-for life, with a condo on the water and a Jeep and a Lexus in the driveway. She was Hector Blanco's mistress. She gave Hank information that helped someone else kill Hector as he returned from Prague on a rainy night a little over a year ago.

At the time, Hank didn't know that chain of events he helped set off would lead him here to kill a woman named Isabel. He knew, of course, there'd be another job, another assignment, but he didn't think that far ahead. He didn't do the math. Didn't connect the future dots. He tried hard to forget after each job. It never worked, but he tried like hell. Felt the simple act of trying was cleansing in some small way.

Hank hears the water from the sink in the bathroom stop.

The singing stops as well. There's a buzz, her phone perhaps.

Hank grips and re-grips the blade in his hand while moving toward the door.

Fighting back the flood of emotions ripping through him, he forces one foot in front of another. Taking in a deep breath, he shuts his eyes tight, then fires them open, trying to force some manner of focus. He's thought about this being the last one. His last job. The last woman he's assigned to. Doesn't know how he'll end it, but this one might break him. The cracks are forming fast. Spreading. Each step toward the bathroom is removing a piece of him.

A flash of her dead body enters his mind.

A pool of blood beneath her.

His imagination is so vivid because he's seen it many times before. The looks on their faces. The shock. The betrayal. Their last thought being them knowing Hank wasn't who they thought he was. *Lady-Killer*. That's what they've tagged him at the Agency.

Shuddering, he shakes his head and braces himself, placing a hand on the wall. He hasn't reached the door yet, but the idea of what he's about to do is peeling away at him. For the first time, he's not sure he can to this.

The thought of her looking up at him. Looking for help, for answers that will never come. Her lifeless eyes staring up at the ceiling.

This is the last one, he tells himself.

Forcing his feet to move forward, he's now in front of the door. As if working on pure muscle memory, he spreads his feet shoulder width, his right foot slightly back, creating a stable foundation. Grinding his teeth, he holds the blade low by his side with his elbow bent, ready to fire it forward like a piston. He wants to strike her fast, make this as painless as possible.

He just wants this to be over.

For both of them. He tried to have himself removed from the job. Hank was having feelings for her. He never told them that, but he's sure they knew. They know everything. They told him that he was already too embedded, that there was no way they'd get another chance. There was a narrative in place, a ready to go story to run with upon her death. A series of dominoes were set to fall. Assets were in place for when the power vacuum opened up. When Isabel "Angel of Death" Blanco was dead.

Yes, Isabel is going to stay with him for a long time.

Hank wipes the moisture from his eyes with the back of his free hand. He thinks of her children, the children whose lives he's going to change forever. Ones who will never know their mother or father. He hopes they have a chance in this world.

The door opens.

Isabel has tears filling her eyes as well. She also has a gun held tight in her shaking hand.

Hank looks at the silencer attached to the barrel of a 9mm Beretta. He glances to her phone on the counter. The screen is still lit up. She just communicated with someone. He heard the buzz. He's going soft. He knows there will be others here in no time.

She knew, he thinks.

Or she was unsure, at least.

This is why she wanted the hotel this time and not their normal secret hideaway house. She knew this was their last night. Or maybe she wanted to be sure of something, something confirmed from that call she just received. Maybe there was something she was waiting to understand before she gave the order.

He'll never know.

Hank knows he has to move fast. Her people will want to take him alive. They'll want to make an example of him. They'll want his death to be messy, just as the Agency told him to be with hers. Same thought process, different sides.

Isabel simply looks at him with her big, beautiful, brutal eyes. Both filled to the brink, waiting to release the flood down her face. She won't let them.

"Sorry," Hank says, barely above a whisper.

She nods.

She raises the gun, her finger tight on the trigger. Hank grabs her wrist and shoves her hand, clearing her aim away from his face. A whisper-blast cuts the air then plunks harmlessly into the far wall with a plume of plaster. Isabel kicks hard, jamming the heel of her bare foot into his knee with a crunch, knocking him off balance, then slams her knee into his stomach, folding him in half.

She adjusts her aim to the back of his head.

Hank spins clear, landing with his back hitting the wall with a thud. A picture drops, crashing to the tile. Her bullets rip into the bed with a bloom of fabric and cotton. There's a rattle at the door. Someone is trying to come in. Isabel turns her gun on him again. Hank's muscle memory kicks in.

He jams his blade into her throat. Blood spits then spills into a pour.

Isabel's eyes go wide. Her lifeless arm drops to her side as she squeezes another blast into the bed before her body wilts down to the tile that's pooling with her blood. Hank holds the blade, watching the life leave her body. He wants to hold her. Comfort her during these final seconds.

The door kicks in.

Three large men in suits storm in with guns raised. Hank flips the blade like a dart. The razor-sharp tactical blade sticks into the throat of the lead bodyguard. Falling to his knees, gasping for air, he flops to the floor. Hushed bullets zip over Hank's head as drops down, then comes up fast with Isabel's gun in his hand.

He fires whispered shots as calmly as can be.

Two bullets.

Two bodyguards drop.

As Hank puts on his shoes, he thinks the bodyguards probably help the narrative. He hates that this is how he's thinking right now. He's also thinking about the layout of the hotel. About how he planned for a quick exit where little to no one will see him. He pulls his cap down low, then squeezes his fists tight to control the shaking. His brain is working on muscle memory. Working the plan as trained to do. He knows the psychological beating will come later. It always does. Those are sneakier. They hit harder and don't give up or die.

Moving toward the door, he stops, fights looking back to Isabel.

He looks anyway.

Something shines around her neck. He can't believe he never noticed it before now, but there just out the reach of her wound is what looks like a silver necklace.

An oddly shaped pendant.

A half of a heart.

Hank opens the car door.

He slips into the leather of the passenger seat. There is no place he'd rather not be more. No other person he'd rather not be near. The strange sensation of wanting to peel his skin off, away from his bones, crawls over him. The desire to slip out from the shell he's trapped himself in and become something different. Something far away from what he's become.

He holds his hands together in his lap. Swallows hard as the sound of Beethoven fills his ears. The glow of the dashboard provides a green filter to the world. The inside of the car feels unworldly. The normally beautiful progression of strings are nails on a chalkboard. The normally comfortable luxury sedan seems like a coffin.

Finally, Hank looks to his left.

As he does, it occurs to him that he doesn't even know the driver's real name.

The Man in the Dark Suit sits behind the wheel, nursing a steaming cup of coffee. He reaches over, turning down the classical station, then glances to Hank. Studies him. Hank's face is drained. There's a slight spray of dried blood across his jaw and check.

"We good?" the Man in the Dark Suit asks, checking his rearview mirror. Quick glances between it and the side mirrors, making sure no one followed Hank.

Hank says nothing. He watches the green glow swallow the Man in the Dark Suit's face. He seems to be even less human than normal. As if the light has removed any quality to his features that might confuse him with a person.

"Are we good?" he asks again.

Hank nods.

"Great." Zero enthusiasm. "Really good to hear." The Dark Suit pulls a workout bag from the back seat, dropping it in Hank's lap. "We'll give it a little more time after this one. We know—"

"What's going to happen to the kids?"

"What?"

"Her kids. The children. The girl and the boy. What is going to happen to them?"

The Man in the Dark Suit stops himself from saying what he was going to say. Reconsiders. Looks Hank over, checking his eyes, trying to get a read on him. *Where's this man's head at?* He picks over his available words carefully before speaking, knowing Hank is a dangerous man in a fragile state. The wrong answer here could be highly problematic.

For everyone.

"It's going to be hard for them. Not going to lie to you. They've lost both their parents and there's not an easy answer for that. But, they have an aunt and uncle in town who are both clean. No ties to that ugly business of hers."

Hank looks at the bag. He doesn't want to take it,

doesn't want the blood money, but he knows he needs it. Knows he needs every penny of it if he's going to disappear. And the decision to disappear was made the second Isabel died.

Hank just didn't know it until now.

Until he looked at the Man in the Dark Suit.

In that fraction of a second, he saw what happens to people in the Agency. He doesn't know much about this man, but he imagines he was once like Hank. Was once a normal person. Had a normal childhood perhaps. Much like anyone else. Then something brought him to the Agency and over the years it's changed him. Didn't happen all at once. Pieces were cut and pulled away over time. Moral compromises were made. A slip here and there, and before you know it, here you are.

A subset of human.

"Those kids will go through a rough patch, no doubt." The Man in the Dark Suit sips his coffee. "But in the end they'll be fine. That life they were headed toward was much rougher. Darker. More dangerous. It's hard to think about it this way, difficult to see it right now I know, but they are better off."

Hank thinks about killing him where he sits.

Thinks about snapping his neck.

Feeling the crack in his hands.

Dumping the body.

But he doesn't.

In a strange way, he knows there's some truth in what he said. Or does he merely hope there is? Are Hank's defenses looking for a reason to let him off the hook? Trying to convince him the world is better off without her? Hank the hero, who has saved humanity, actually doing the children a favor by being a major part in the deaths of their parents.

The bullshit is so deep he can't begin to breathe.

Back to thinking about snapping his neck.

"Something else on your mind?" the Man in the Dark Suit asks, looking toward Hank while messing with the cheap coffee cup lid.

"She had some people." Hank stares out the windshield, avoiding eye contact. "They came into the room with guns. She knew something was up."

"Bodyguards?"

Hank nods.

"You take care of them?"

Hank nods.

"Well, don't worry about any of that. We'll do our thing. Clean it up per usual." Dark Suit looks to him. "You concerned they're onto you? That the thing?"

Hank opens the door, exits without saying another word.

Hank drops down into the plush window seat.

A window seat in first class. He's showered, dressed in a black T-shirt and jeans. The ticket and the clothes were in the bag, along with the money. Lots of it. A little extra this time. Hank didn't realize the Agency was in the business of giving sentimentality bonus money.

His blood-money bonus.

Sipping a whiskey, he closes his eyes, trying to hit reset on everything. Reshuffle the world. Hoping for a better view of things. He cried in the shower at his motel. Hasn't cried since he doesn't know when. He thought it'd make him feel better for some reason. It didn't. He's hoping the whiskey will be more successful. He knows it won't. The whiskey does his favorite burn, however, letting his brain unclench some, if only for a moment. His mind flips and turns like a high-speed car wreck, helplessly flailing into the night. The last few years play over and over again behind his eyes. A continuous stream of images and motion he'd rather not revisit. Violent, dirty deeds all committed by his own hand.

He asks for another drink.

Thoughts of quitting this life have surfaced before. Usually right after a job. Then they fade away after a day or two of drinking. After sufficient numbing time has passed. Then, later, he'd meet with the Man in the Dark Suit, get an assignment and get into character. There was always the odd spark of the challenge in the beginning. Like he blocked out the fact that the challenge always ended with ending someone's life. Slipping into another skin has helped him shake loose the guilt, if he's being honest. *It wasn't me, it was that other guy.* He's drifted in and out of these roles so often he doesn't remember the details of all of them. A faceless lady-killer armed with smiles and weaponized conversation.

There are some constants for each part he's played.

The role of charming, seductive male is one he's been trained to do, but he's been somewhat of a natural all his life. Used to entertain the family table at Christmas dinner. He'd put on shows as a child. Keep the girls gooey-eyed and laughing in high school.

Hank counts seven in all.

Seven women he's lied to, laughed with, conned into caring about him, and then killed.

This needs to end.

Someone else can and will do it. At least it won't be him taking the lives. There's little comfort in that reality, but little comfort is far better than none at all.

Isabel was different.

She got to him.

Discipline got him through most of the seven. Discipline, along with the grand idea he was doing some good for God and Country. That he was helping people by what he was doing. And perhaps that was true. But even Hank the Lady-Killer can't deny good old-fashioned physical attraction mixed with the pure enjoyment of being a part of something electric. That's what they were together. Electric. She was funny, strong and wicked in a very magnetic way. They had a connection. An undeniable spark the moment they met. She had done bad, horrible things. But so had Hank. They shared a sense of humor and common view of life, and they simply loved being around one another.

Right or wrong.

Those are the facts.

Hank picks up a rental car near JFK and heads toward the Bronx.

The whiskey was just enough to remove the layer of stress. At a gas station, he places the nozzle through the backseat window instead of into the tank. He checks to make sure no one is watching while keeping his back toward the lone camera aimed at the pump. The security camera at the cashier has a bad angle on the car and won't be able to catch Hank and what he's doing. Made sure to use one of the prepaid credit cards from the bag the Agency gave him at the pump. He knows damn well those are all tracked, so he'll have to dump them, but he wants the Agency to see some sort of trail. Wants them to trace him to here.

Hank's creating a narrative too.

Soon enough, he'll become a ghost. Far away, nowhere near here.

The gas pours over the seat and floorboard. Not a ton, but enough to do the job.

There's a stretch of road, a street not far from here, where he'll torch the car. It's perfect. A place Hank has known for years for various other reasons. It's populated, but not so much so that he won't have enough time to run a few streets over as the car burns to steal a new one. He'll torch that one a few states later, then steal another car and press repeat.

He hopes to stir up some chaos. It'll help him first slip out of town, then out into nothing.

The quick analysis dictates it'll take three cars to get him where he needs to go. There's a stop along the way he'll have to make. He'll need to keep his speed low and stay off the main roads. He's got some cash and guns stashed about nine and half hours from here by car. He had an assignment there last year. Amy was her name, he thinks. Maybe it was Alison. He doesn't even remember why he stashed that care package there last year. Maybe he was planning his escape even while blind drunk.

He pulls the nozzle back, slipping it out from the back window of the rental car.

The pieces of this plan have been in place for a while. Jumbled. Not connected. He didn't pull them all together until the night before Isabel. If he's being honest, he didn't finalize it until he was in the car with the Man in the Dark Suit. The idea of meeting up with that man again in about month or so at some coffee shop or at the top of some parking garage somewhere is not something Hank wants to live through. Sitting in a car at some dock or in some alley or in some field in nowhere USA listening to him describe a new woman Hank needs to lie to and murder. That's not something Hank can abide any longer.

They will look for him.

Of course they will.

The Agency will hunt far and wide.

Hank rolls down the window as he drives off from the station. The smell of the gas is almost unbearable, but he doesn't have far to go. He pulls a new small tactical blade from his bag and cuts his finger. He grips the wheel tight, letting the blood spread around the wheel. He wants it there. He wipes his blood on the seat, the dash. When he stops, he'll rub his bloody fingers across the door and sides of the car. He wants his DNA found. He knows the car will burn from the backseat awhile before the entire car goes up. He also knows that the people who will look for him can pull DNA from just about anything, anywhere. The fire will destroy some of the evidence of him being there, but not all of it.

He'll light the car on fire, fire a few shots from his gun out into the night air and a couple of blasts inside and outside the car. Then he'll run like hell a few blocks over and steal that first car. It's a sad state of affairs when it's easier to steal a car than avoid cameras at the subways or train stations. Less complicated than sidestepping eyeball witnesses from cabs or Uber. He has some fake license plates, burn plates he got from a guy not associated with the Agency. He can use them here and there to buy himself some much-needed time.

Getting out of the city will be the trickiest, most stressful time. The hold your breath time with the most electric and human eyes to avoid. Many possible points of failure, but once he clears the greater New York area his odds of success increase dramatically. He's already thought of two towns that would be perfect for him to disappear into. Two tiny towns that are potential homes for Henry "Hank" Kane. One in Colorado and one in Texas. It will be tense, but the entire transformation should only take a hard-fought day or so.

Hank knows the math of becoming a ghost.

The narrative he's constructing will be that Isabel's

people got to him. There was a struggle. Little bit of gunplay. They'll find some blood from Hank on the car, the bullet holes, and surmise those drug lord animals lit the car up and dragged Hank somewhere to meet his brutal death. Not hard to put a story together or to imagine one, considering they almost got him at the hotel. He made sure the Dark Suit got that detail before he left him in his car. Even got him to create the question in his own mind.

"You concerned they're onto you? That the thing?"

The Agency will track the card he used at the pump.

They will find the car.

They will find his blood.

Hopefully, they will never find Hank in Rough Creek, Texas.

Hank and Becky Rant drive all night.

Hank hasn't said more than a handful of words the entire trip. He's a silent wall, driving getaway after burning his house and business down to the ground in the blink of an eye. Becky Rant rides shotgun, thinking about it all but not feeling that any of it is strange. Strange is a label she does not apply to her life. Strange is expected.

A steady state of crazy.

Becky Rant knows he has questions about her. Of course he does. She has questions too, a mountain of them. Early on in the drive, while leaving Texas, she thought of asking him *why*. Asking him why he burned everything down, wanting to know if he did it for her or if there was something else. She can guess. She knows a lot about him, but not everything. It's obvious he had things in place so he could operate at a moment's notice. The speed at which he progressed was nothing short of remarkable. An exit strategy at the ready. But what was the trigger?

That is what she wanted to know during their pedal to the floor, mid-morning escape from Rough Creek. Still wants to know now.

"Why did you do that?" she asks.

He comes back with, "Why did I do what?" Perhaps buying himself time to think up a lie as his eyes focus hard on the road out of town.

"*What?*" She laughs. "Oh I don't know, why did you light your life on fire?"

"Felt I didn't have much of choice."

Becky Rant blinks, watching the world blur by out the window. She understands his response based on what she knows, but he doesn't know what she knows, so she needs to still play the part. A part that she's getting more and more weary of playing. Dragging info out of him is getting beyond tiring and needs to end.

Soon.

"Gonna need a little more than that."

"No." He shakes his head then glances her way briefly.

There was just the simple flash of his tired eyes, but

it stopped her. Froze her mouth closed and pressed pause on her heartbeat. The undeniable restrained anger held back behind those eyes was almost enough for Becky Rant to jump out the truck.

"No," he says again softly, tightening his fingers around the steering wheel, looking straight at the road ahead of them. "Let's think about what we want to say to one another. We have a drive ahead of us. Hours and hours to go. To where, I'm not sure. I have a couple of ideas. But let's you and me really think about what we want to say. What we need to say."

She looks his way, but not too long, not sure she wants to open the door to what he's thinking. Nodding, she whispers a gentle *okay,* letting him know that she gets it. She allows the silence to fill up the cab of the truck. The sound of the tires gripping the road provide the only soundtrack to their thoughts. She has a lot to sift through in her mind. He was right, as much as she hated to admit it. Firing off everything bouncing in her head, unloading all that she wants to say, the vomiting of nouns, verbs and adjectives fueled by emotion, would more likely hurt than help. Not the best way to go.

"Fine," she finally says. "You're going first, though."

Hank allows a smirk, then shakes his head again. "Unbelievable."

Becky Rant smiles, pauses, then reaches out to hold his hand.

Not sure why. Felt she needed to, she guesses.

He lets her for a moment. The feeling of her fingers wrapped in his feels nice. He enjoys the connection with another person, a sensation he'd almost forgotten. The simplicity of a person's touch is powerful. Something that gets lost in today's world. The simple schoolboy act of holding a girl's hand is something Hank has always loved.

His mind shifts to thoughts of holding Isabel's hand on the beach. Walking and laughing with their hands locked and their toes digging into the warm sand. He remembered loving the feel of it. The warmth inside of him. The silence of an understood affection.

Hank shakes his fingers loose from Becky Rant's, pulling back as if she were carrying a disease. He offers no explanation or comforting words. Only cold silence. Becky Rant draws a quick breath as his fingers rip away from hers. The truck gets unbearably quiet. It's like the temperature dropped twenty degrees in the cab as well. The silence is deafening.

"We need to get a new car," he says.

"Okay."

"Soon."

They steal a new car in New Mexico and don't say word to one another for the rest of the ride to Colorado.

They stop and pick a tiny motel in a small town off the beaten path in southern Colorado, swallowed by trees and seemingly endless natural beauty. Wooden bears and families on vacation occupy the place, but there was still a disorienting feeling of being on another planet. They got a room on the first floor, corner spot with good sight lines. Hank fails to mention this was one of the towns he considered moving to when he disappeared.

They drop their bags.

They sit on two beds facing one another in a small motel room in southern Colorado with bears and woodsy-crap on the walls. Becky Rant realizes she doesn't even know the name of the town they've landed in. Doesn't matter, because tomorrow morning they will move on. She doesn't know where. Not sure he does either. She thinks a lot of that depends on the conversation that is about to take place.

She's not sure if they will both live through it.

Both are capable of bad things.

Hank drags a small table over from the window and sets it between them. He disappears into the bathroom for a second, without a word or a look. She wants to ask him what's going on, but stops herself. She wants Hank to speak first. Being silent for these many hours has indeed given her time to think about what to say. Problem is, she still has no idea what words to use. The subjects are clear; it's the execution of the idea that is at issue. She needs to get that mix right, or everything is lost.

He's had a lot of time to think as well. Time to work through what he knows.

This is the great unknown for Becky Rant.

What he knows and doesn't know could be the difference between her plan working out or Hank putting a bullet in her brain. He could come out of that bathroom with a gun and take her out right now. She saw the file of what he did to the woman in Cardiff-by-the-Sea. She has no choice but to wait. She does, however, reach into her bag that rests at her feet. Removing her 9mm, her eyes dance. She needs to make a decision. Holding the gun in hand when he comes out is the wrong play, but she knows she wants it close to her. She slides it under a pillow next to her, then adjusts the flat, cheap motel pillow even closer.

The situation is complex, at best.

Hank steps out from the bathroom.

He's holding something behind his back. Becky Rant

holds her breath, slipping her hand slowly under the pillow, never breaking eye contact.

She swallows, wets her dry lips.

Hank pulls his arm around.

Her hand grips the gun under the pillow. As she pulls her arm forward, she eyes his hand.

"Found this in your room in Texas." Hank holds out a bottle of whiskey. It's one of her bottles of Dewar's. "Before, ya know."

"You lit it on fire."

He shrugs. "You ready?" He cracks the cap, raising his eyebrows. "Ready to talk?"

Becky Rant exhales, releases her grip on the gun, and slides her hand out from under the pillow. She keeps her fingers on the bed, ready if needed.

"You want to put that gun on the table?" he asks, grabbing two plastic cups sitting by the ice bucket. "Might make things easier on you, Quick Draw Becky."

She rolls her eyes. *Smug son of a bitch.*

"Just trying to take care of myself." She picks up the pillow with a sigh and a defeated smirk. Not wanting to be an idiot about the situation, she slides her gun next to her thigh.

Taking a seat on the bed across from her, he sets down the two cups, then pours two snorts about two fingers high. He pushes a cup toward her. It's not lost on her that he made sure that she saw him crack the cap and pour the drinks in front of her. Making sure she knows that he didn't slip anything freaky into the drinks. It's an act of showing she can trust him. It's a start, she thinks, but she'll relax later. If warranted.

"Think you wanted me to start?" He takes a drink.

She nods, downing the entire cup.

He refills. Three fingers this time.

"Where should I start?" he asks.

"Shortly after your birth."

"Funny." He drinks again. "I'll keep it to the good parts. I am—I was—an operator within the Agency. I have a feeling you know what I mean by that, but if you don't, it's a fancy way of saying I killed people when asked by government employees in suits." He waits for a reaction from her.

Testing her.

Becky Rant drinks but says nothing. She pours four fingers.

"Am I right? You knew all that, didn't you?"

She nods, then reaches into her bag on instinct, searches, finds one of her bottles of pills. She wants nothing more than to pop a bit of Oxy in her mouth. Let it go to work on her personal chemistry. She doesn't. She stops just short, but leaves the bottle out for comfort. She motions for him to keep going. Hank eyes the bottle of pills.

"May I?" he asks, holding a hand out toward the bottle.

"No." She knows he's had his struggles with pills too. "Need you to hold it together. We'll have to settle for whiskey."

He nods, pulling his hand back.

"I was a Marine." He tips his plastic cup to her. "A good one. Did you know that?"

She gives a single nod, tipping her cup his way, returning the gesture.

"I'm from a small town, much like Rough Creek. Joined the Marines after high school." His eyes glaze over while working through his story. "They came to me after basic. I did well. Tested high. They came to me on graduation day. Family Day, they called it. The Agency knew I had no family, but they kept calling it Family Day over and over again. Really wanting that to dig into me." He drinks. "I fit a profile they wanted. They were convincing sales people. I went into new training."

There's a wide-open vulnerability to the look spreading across his face. The tone he's using, his voice, his entire posture has changed. Becky Rant can't deny that he's trying to ease the weight of what he's been dragging around. Dying to drop it to the floor, if only for a little while. She sees his hands tremble as he talks.

Becky Rant pours him more, moving to the bed next to him.

Hank stares out into nothing, barely noticing that she has moved closer. His mind pours out as he speaks. An unloading process he's kept bottled up for a long, long time. He's not sure he's ever said these things out loud before, to anyone. Even to himself when alone. Not sure he's ever thought this all through before now. He's never connected all the dots of his life until now. The pain of a truthful timeline is hard to view in its entirety.

"I was trained to gain the trust of female assets, gather information, and eliminate them when told." His hands shake more noticeably now. Tears form in the corners of his eyes.

Becky Rant says nothing. Listens. It hurts to see him like this. Knowing what she knows and hearing him say the words is tough to watch. The look in his eyes. The pain in his voice. He's setting down a heavy weight he's been carrying.

"There were a lot of them," he says.

She touches his hand.

"There was one..."

A cold spike shoots through her.

"One that broke me in half. She... she was a hard one. What I did to her..."

As his voice trails off, he takes another drink, then pours himself another. She wants to stop him going forward, but needs to let him continue. Needs to see him talk about it. Needs to see the look on his face. To hear it come from his mouth.

Hank closes his eyes.

She can see he's shutting down. *We're quite a pair*, she thinks, taking a slug of whiskey then touching her necklace, rubbing the half-heart between her fingers. *Both faked our own deaths. Both responsible for the death of someone we cared about.*

She holds him gently, this broken, brutal man, resting her head on his shoulder. Squeezing tighter, she feels the tension in his body. He won't look at her, but he's not retreating back into himself either. He keeps talking, unspooling his past for an audience of one.

She knows she has to tell him.

This isn't how she planned it. She thought this man was a simple, cold psychopath. Why would she think otherwise? She counted on it. She was going to beat him at his own game. Seduce him, get him to tell her what she needed to know, then kill him. Do what he did to all of them. What he did to her friend.

Becky Rant didn't plan on Isabel being right about him.

He's a good man in a bad spot, Isabel said to her during brunch one day by the beach. The morning before she died. Isabel had no idea that she was saying those words to the person truly responsible for her death. That her lifelong friend served her up to the wolves.

"I know," Becky Rant whispers, letting her tears drop and roll down his arm. "I know."

She feels Hank's shoulder rise and fall, struggling to hold it together, fighting to be a tough guy. Becky Rant clears her throat.

"My turn?"

Hank nods.

"Okay." She takes a drink. "I need to tell you some things."

Isabel and Becky Rant sit at an oceanside restaurant.

The stretching patio offers an amazing view, looking out over the beach and rolling waves of the Pacific Ocean. Families are out enjoying the day, mixed among bikini visions laid out in the golden sand and beach muscle boys straining to steal any kind of a look. Bicycles ride by and joggers clock their miles among the wonders of seventy-two degrees sunny Southern California.

This has become a favorite brunch spot for Isabel and Becky Rant over the years. One they've been coming to for as long as they've known each other, as adults at least. At least since they could cover the tab. Becky moved to LA a while back, and she doesn't make it down this way as often as she'd like, but she does take the train down along the coast when she can.

The bottoms of the white table cloths rustle in the breeze. Waitstaff buzz in black tie. This is how life should be lived. At least for those who can fit the bill at this gorgeous hotel located on the water. Coffee, thick-cut bacon, fresh-as-hell fruit, and delicate pastries, along with a mimosa for Becky Rant and a Bloody Mary for Isabel.

Life was meant to be good. That phrase was something they always said to one another even when life was complete hell back during their days in the California foster care system.

Becky Rant has never seen her friend out of sorts the way she is today, however. Isabel is normally the steady rock of the two. Emotions kept under lock and key. A woman of steel. Right now, she's different. Right now, this woman of steel is a ball of nervous energy. Isabel, the gorgeous creature of control with the impossible mix of looks, smarts and toughness, is a ball of anxiety. She's someone Becky Rant leaned on ever since they met at the home. Isabel rarely needed to lean, let alone need a lifeline. Isabel is showing a different side right now and Becky Rant isn't sure she likes it. She seems anxious. Edgy even. Anxious and edgy—two words she'd never use to describe her friend.

Lifelong friends, despite the rough terrain their lives have dragged them through, kicking and screaming. There was an immediate connection between them as little girls. They both lost their parents before they were even old enough to remember them. They became sisters to one another, forming a family they would never have under normal circumstances. There was another one they let in, a boy, a brother of sorts. Johnny was what he liked to be called.

They share stories of how Johnny was the one who taught them how to use their fists and how to fight. There was a lot of trial and error. Perhaps more error, but those lessons from Johnny saved them throughout the years. Truth be told, Becky Rant needed it more than Isabel. Isabel was a natural fighter. Becky Rant needed to work at it.

Becky was Maid of Honor when Isabel married Hector. She was there when Isabel's twins were born. There when Isabel buried her husband, then later broke down in private. She held her friend as the tears dropped to the tile of the bathroom floor. Felt Isabel shake and quiver as the sorrow rattled and tore its way through her.

Becky Rant knew her friend had been seeing someone new recently. The first someone since her husband was killed. All Becky Rant knew was that he was good-looking and was *ridiculously good in bed*, according to Isabel. The details were vivid and hot as hell. Isabel loved sharing all the juicy nuances of their time together with her friend. Isabel also talked about how kind he was and how much fun they had together. Made Becky Rant happy to see Isabel like this. To see her friend enjoying herself again at last. Living her life after Hector.

But today there is an uneasiness to her that Becky Rant has not seen in her old friend since their rocky childhood.

Becky Rant has worked in and around Hector's network for the last few years. Helped find information, work a deal here and there, even crack some skulls on occasion. All work that Becky Rant neither loved nor hated; it just was, and it paid well. Not like she chose this life over med school.

Becky Rant's stomach twists into knots the more Isabel talks. There's guilt and self-hatred ripping its way into her. A few months ago—maybe three, could be five, she's lost track—Becky Rant got tagged in a bust. Got leaned on hard by the feds. She became an informant for the Agency. For a while, she was able to hand down a few small-time dirt bags and get away with it while still holding her head high. Still able to hang out with Isabel without giving up their relationship to the Agency.

Keeping their friendship intact and safe from the long, strangling tentacles of the law.

But a man like Ronald Church doesn't play.

At least not for long.

He always knew Becky Rant was holding out on him. An Agency rockstar, he was. He wore her down. Manipulation. Mind games. He got her using again. Booze at first.

I can handle a little drink, right? she told herself.

Then pills. Lots of pills. Her mind became cloudy. A shadow of herself. And in the deepest part of her drug-induced haze she tried sleeping with him in order to control him. An act that had worked for her in the past. It did the opposite, this time.

A master at the game, Ronald slept with her, then told her it was fun but not enough to move the needle. "You're cute, but not that cute," were the words he used. Made sure she felt used and useless. Then he fed her more whiskey and pills. That's when he told her she needed to try harder, and by that he meant he wanted info on her dear old friend.

He'd been after Isabel all along.

Becky Rant fought it like hell. Held him off with many starts and stops. Misled him down wrong paths. Twisted roads. Dead ends. She did her best to spin him in wrong directions. Gave him small jobs, minor, insignificant bits of info. Ronald would smile, nod, and thank her. Then one day he took her foster brother off the street. Her Johnny, who had taught her how to fight all those years ago. She'd told Ronald about him in bed one night while she was high as a kite. At the time, she thought she was sharing with someone she was sleeping with. A relationship of sorts.

She realized quickly she was helping a monster.

Ronald knew then that Johnny was the sore spot for him to press hard. A potential weakness to exploit. Looking back, she realizes that she slow-pitched that one to him. The mental game he was playing, the brutal art of what he did, was cold, but something to admire in a sick sort of way.

One of Ronald's guys gave Johnny a good beating one sunny Tuesday afternoon in the middle of Sunset Boulevard near the 405. Savagely wailed on him to within an inch of his life, all shown to her on a live video feed Ronald forced Becky Rant to watch.

She screamed out for the Man in the Dark Suit to stop, even though he couldn't hear her. Ronald had told the Dark Suit to call him Jonathan as he hurt him. To scream it at him. Yell the name his father gave him, what his father had called him while he beat him as a child. Ronald wanted Dark Suit to say the name over and over, knowing that Johnny hated his given name so much.

Ronald wanted Becky Rant to know what control really looked like. Wanted her to know how to break someone in two.

Even the simple mental trick of using a certain name can land like a hammer. Becky Rant begged for it to stop. Ronald agreed to call it off if she gave him information. Real information. Information on her other friend, Isabel. Schedules. Patterns of her life. More psychological profiling, details about her, rather than hard evidence to build a case.

Seemed somewhat harmless at the time to Becky Rant, considering the business Isabel was in. She was surrounded by protection. Electronic monitoring and heavily-armed muscle on a twenty-four seven rotation. Isabel was the head of an organization as powerful, or maybe more, than the precious Agency Ronald and the Man in the Dark Suit were so proudly a part of. What harm could it do to give him some minor details about someone untouchable?

Later, she'd understand.

Three days passed and Becky Rant found out that Johnny had been shot in the back of the head then dumped in a dumpster off Yucca Street in Hollywood. Ronald texted her the picture. Johnny's lifeless body laid out among the trash. Probably posed just for her. His mouth open wide. His face almost unrecognizable. He looked afraid. It still crushes her when she thinks of it. How afraid Johnny must have been before he died.

That's the genius of someone like Ronald Church.

Not only did he take someone away from her that she cared about, someone close to her from her lonely, broken childhood, but what he also did, an added bonus for Ronald, maybe more important to him, was that he showed her how easily they could beat down her protector. Render him meaningless. How they could remove her childhood bodyguard from the earth in the blink of an eye. The very someone who taught Becky Rant how to fight. How to defend herself from the big, bad world. Stripping away her confidence. Jarring her sense of physical safety. Shaking her to the core.

A cool breeze blows off the ocean, snapping Becky Rant back into the here and now.

Isabel fidgets. Bites the inside of her cheek. For the third time in the ten seconds, Isabel picks up her napkin then sets it back down in her lap.

Becky Rant asks, "You okay?"

"Yeah, why?"

"You seem a little off."

"Do I now?"

"Yeah." Becky Rant chews on a slab of bacon. "Yeah, ya do."

Isabel takes a drink, then touches Becky Rant's hand. "I need to ask you for a favor."

She's never asked her for anything in her life. Never needed anything from her. Becky Rant nods, trying to hide the concern that's bubbling up inside of her. She stares at the half-heart necklace, the right side of the heart dangling from Isabel's neck.

"What are you talking about?" Becky Rant asks.

"There's something going on. I'm not sure. People might be on me. It's crazy."

Becky Rant's blood runs cold. She knows the information she's given Ronald Church.

"People are always on you, Bel," she says, touching the left side of the heart around her neck. "What's so different now?"

"Little signs for things not being right. I feel it. Things are off." Isabel looks around. "Not sure who to trust." She closes her eyes, as if talking to herself. "I might have let the wrong one in. I don't know." Her eyes open, but she's not looking at anything. "I don't know for sure. I hope I'm wrong. I've got some people looking into him. Damn I hope I'm wrong."

Becky Rant's heart pounds against her ribs. Her stomach drops. She knows what's happening, knows in the pit of her soul that Ronald has put someone on Isabel. He put this new guy into her life. That's why he wanted all that information from her. That particular type of information. He knew how to piece together the bits that Becky Rant fed him. He was building a profile. The booze and pills had dulled her to the point of becoming a pile of dust.

She can't believe she's done this to Isabel.

To herself.

"I don't understand," Becky Rant says, trying to get more out of her friend.

But she does understand. She understands too damn well. She wants to scream across the table. Tell her to run. Take her friend by the hand and go running like hell to that off-the-books house Isabel talks about all the time, wherever it is, the one she's been taking this new man to for their little getaways. Isabel said she takes him there to protect him. Didn't want to get him mixed up in her business.

Becky wants to hold Isabel's beautiful face in her hands and tell her she's sorry.

"Look. Hear me on this." Isabel sips her Bloody Mary and motions to her bodyguard standing at the other end of the patio while continuing the conversation. "It's going to be okay, but if it goes the wrong way promise me you'll do what you've agreed to do."

It feels like a knife slicing across her insides. Becky Rant can't even find the words to say. She is godmother to Isabel's children. Something they both take very seriously, though Becky Rant hasn't thought much about it lately. Maybe she should have before now. The drugs and booze have made her weak beyond reason. Once Hector was killed, she should have thought more about her responsibilities and implications. Her promises. Hard promises you don't worm out of.

What have I done?

Then it hits her like a sledgehammer.

She struggles to remember what Ronald said. What he said about a man who works special assignments, shadowy assignments. He was drunk, she was high, and he was bragging about what a big deal he was in the Agency. *Ronald Church, the baddest man alive* type of crap. Endless stories of how great and mighty Ronald Church was. He mentioned someone they called *Lady-Killer*, someone who worked his way into the lives of female targets for the Agency. For some reason, Ronald found it funny the Lady-Killer always went by a series of names that began with S—Scott, Sammy, Steve...

"What's his name?" Becky Rant asks with bite.

"Who?"

"Your new guy. What's his name?"

"Stephen. Why?"

Becky Rant drops her fork, letting it clank and rattle on the plate. Isabel gives her a strange look as her cell goes off, buzz-jumping on the tablecloth. Her eyes widen, seeing the number. She holds up a finger, taking the call away from the table. Her bodyguards take their places covering the entry and exit points. Standard security operating protocol.

Becky Rant fights to find her breathing. She can't believe it. Ronald used her to help setup Isabel with a killer. The personal questions, questions about her husband, her likes and dislikes, the girl talk and the locations. The schedule she keeps. Ronald used all of it to set Isabel up for her own murder. A date with a monster.

Isabel smiles and laughs while on the call.

Is she on the phone with him right now?

Becky Rant doesn't know what to do. She gets up, moves toward Isabel, about to stop her, end the conversation and tell her everything. Come clean with it all. Let all the ugliness fall, anything to stop what's happening.

They can still run. They've always been able to run.

From the corner of her eye, she sees the Man in the Dark Suit sitting alone sipping coffee a few tables over from them. He's one of Ronald's people. One of his worst people. The one who beat Johnny. Probably the one who shot him and left his body in that Hollywood dumpster. The Dark Suit gives her an ever so slight wink before turning his attention to the ocean.

She wants to disappear. Wants the earth to open up and swallow her whole.

Isabel steps over to her. She's visibly in a hurry, but hugs her friend tight and holds her longer than usual. Becky Rant wants to tell her right now, to confess, but can't find the words. Her tongue fumbles inside of her mouth. Unspoken words catch in her throat.

Isabel talks, but Becky Rant can barely hear. Fragments about how everything is going to be fine and that she will call her tomorrow. She's meeting Stephen at a nice hotel. Isabel pulls back and looks her in the eye.

"I'll be sure about him tonight," she says.

Becky Rant can't take her eyes off the right side of the heart hanging from Isabel's neck that has the letters ST and CHES on it. She remembers when they bought the cheap necklace at the mall when they were stupid teenagers. They were a combination of scared and tough at the same time. Strong and insanely weak, not able, or not willing, to tackle the world like other people. They decided Becky would take the left side and Isabel the right.

Isabel kisses her on the cheek, then disappears from the patios with her bodyguards clearing the way for her while watching her blind spots.

Only Becky Rant knows they're missing a big one in a dark suit.

Becky Rant wants to break down on the patio, to collapse into a puddle. She rubs the left side of the heart around her neck. Her half with BE and BIT engraved on it. Thinking back again to the small store in that tacky mall in the valley, she remembers paying in quarters and nickels. It was all they had between them and they used it to buy this stupid necklace. The waves of giggles they split up the words on the heart: *BEST BITCHES*.

The silly pride they took in the statement it made.

Becky Rant hears a throat clear. She knows who it is.

The Man in the Dark Suit can go fuck himself.

7 DAYS AGO (SOMEWHERE, COLORADO)

Becky Rant sits with her eyes forward, her head still resting on Hank's shoulder.

They've been sipping Dewar's while she told Hank about that morning on the patio with Isabel. She thought long and hard about how to tell him. The drive out of Texas gave her plenty of time to decide. She didn't want a longwinded explanation of the entirety of her and Isabel's relationship. Way too much to cover. After miles of internal debate, Becky Rant decided the story about their last brunch in San Diego was best. It wrapped up everything in one story. It was painful as hell to talk about, to let out, especially with him, but she didn't see any other way this was going to work. She had to go backward to move forward.

He needed to know.

He hasn't said a word.

She hasn't removed her head from his shoulder for more than a second, only long enough to take a drink and refill their cups.

He let her talk uninterrupted for what seemed like hours, though she knows it was only minutes. She doesn't know him incredibly well, but knows enough to give him space. To allow him the time to digest the information. The only sound in the room is their breathing and the low hum of a TV next door.

Hank slips his gun out from behind his back.

Becky Rant's heart skips a row of beats. Her head springs off his shoulder.

Hank tosses the gun over to the other bed. They watch it land with a bounce on the cheap mattress. Before she can register what's happening, Hank has taken the gun she's kept next to her and tosses it over to the bed, landing inches from his. He gently touches her faces, moving her head back to his shoulder. They sit in silence again. Sipping their whiskey.

"You done?" he finally asks.

"Yes," she says, a crack in her voice.

"My turn again?"

"Yes."

"You asked me why I burned down the house, the motel."

"I did."

"You put that necklace on at the bar. I didn't see it before then. Not sure you were wearing it before. I've seen the other half of it. Saw Isabel wearing it."

Becky Rant closes her eyes.

Half embarrassed for not thinking about that, half grateful she didn't.

"The second I saw it, I knew at least part of your *why*. Why you wanted to find me so bad."

"Oh hell." She sighs. "That damn obvious?"

"I'd love to think attractive women roll into Rough Creek all the time to try to seduce me, but I know that shit ain't the truth."

"Well, I mean, you're a good-looking man with some charm. It's not like—"

"Stop."

"Fine."

"I saw the necklace and knew you were somehow linked to Isabel. That meant you were either with the Agency or her business partners, and neither of those are known for compassion, nor are they famous for giving second chances. Those people think I'm dead. I needed to erase any trace of me being there."

Becky Rant takes a sip. She wants to say so much, but knows to let him keep going.

"How did you find me?"

"Mostly luck. I pieced together things Isabel told me and what I found out about you from Ronald—"

"Ronald Church?"

"That's the chap."

"He's a piece of shit."

"True."

Hank takes a gulp of whiskey, wanting to ask how she's connect to someone like Ronald Church, to ask if she's sleeping with him. He decides he'd rather not know.

"Isabel said you talked about missing the simplicity of small towns. Your childhood. That you talked about Texas once." She clears her throat. "I guessed the date you disappeared from the Agency. Overheard some conversations Ronald had. Watched his mood go all to hell. I made a list of small towns in Texas that might work for you. Got lucky and found that a house sold in Rough Creek around the time you checked out. Real estate doesn't move in small towns like larger cities. That nice real estate agent, Meredith, was very chatty. Thought you were a hottie."

"Dammit, Meredith."

Becky Rant smiles. She's starting to relax, probably because of the whiskey, but mainly because she's fairly certain Hank isn't going to slit her throat and eat her heart.

He asks about the twins. About Isabel's children.

Becky Rant breathes in deep then takes her head off his shoulder. She forces him to look at her. She needs him to hear everything she has to say. This point needs to be perfectly clear. Needs to stick on a personal level.

"They're fine, for now. They, the Agency, they know I'm the legal guardian and godmother, and that's not good for the children, or me."

"Who's with them now?"

"Two kindly old ladies who do some work as nannies. I scraped up as much money as I could, but I can't pay them plus the rent on the place they're hiding in for much longer. I told them to keep the babies inside, that they have rare skin conditions and need to avoid the sun."

"Smart."

"Thanks." She takes a long drink. "I need your help."

"No shit."

"No more games. No more bullshit. Okay?"

Hank nods.

"Ronald, the Agency, they'll want to use those children as some kind of leverage. Trade them both for something else in the cartels. I can't have that."

She locks into his eyes.

"Those children. They didn't do a damn thing wrong. You, me, Isabel... We're guilty as hell of all kinds of wrong. Can't speak for you, but I've made a mountain of mistakes that almost buried me alive. I'm working damn hard to be better. I am. I gotta own my baggage. The things I've done. The things that have brought me here."

Her intensity rips up a notch with each word.

"Those kids didn't do anything to anybody. They have a shot. I'm not letting their lives be decided by those animals, and I'm sure as hell not letting those babies get tossed into the goddamn foster care system. Not to mention..." She pauses. Catches her breath. Wipes her eyes. "I made a promise."

Hank's face is solemn, but there's a full-on storm raging behind that mask.

"You know the address of a house," she says. "A place that can help me help them."

"Where?"

"You and Isabel used to go there."

"Okay." Hank thinks, processing. "Question?"

"Shoot."

"How do you plan on taking care of these kids if the most resourceful murderers on the planet are after you?"

Becky Rant grins, drinks straight from the bottle this time.

"Because, Hank Kane, much like you, I'm dead too."

11 DAYS AGO (LOS ANGELES)

The second she found out Isabel had been killed, Becky Rant knew.

Knew Ronald was going to take her out.

No reason to keep her around as a loose end. He'd gotten what he wanted out of her. Twisted her life and manipulated her into nothing but a broken bag of bones. The drugs, the booze, the mind games had all taken a heavy toll, but she knew she needed to buy herself some time. Some time to get ready. Some time to get her head right and get her body in shape for what she needed to do.

Ronald didn't know it, but he lit a fire in her.

One she'd forgotten.

One that had been masked by his pills and toxic words.

Once she got Isabel's children safely stashed with the kindly nannies, she created a list. Jotted it down on her little peach to-do pad. Every box has been checked on the path to her death, but there's one last one.

A big one.

She always knew dying would be the hardest part.

She knew she couldn't wait to see how Ronald was going to kill her. And she knew that now that Isabel was out of the way he would do it quickly. So, she swallowed her tears and pulled off the acting job of the century. She pretended she had no idea what had happened. No clue what he did to her lifelong friend. Knew nothing about the Lady-Killer and how she served her up to him.

Becky Rant needed to bait a hook, cast a line into the water.

She casually mentioned a house Isabel had off the books.

Ronald Church's ears perked up.

She went on to say she wasn't sure, but she thought it might be Isabel's "in case of emergency" house. Something that contained getaway type money and other items that would help someone disappear. This was true. Isabel took *Stephen* there, but no one but Becky Rant knew exactly what the place was. Isabel knew it was a risk to take her lover there, but she wanted to protect him and that house was the closest thing to absolute privacy she had in this world.

Becky Rant pressed on with her story, asking Ronald to imagine the kind of cash it would take for someone like Isabel to disappear. *Must be astronomical.*

She could see Ronald's mind grind on that. Could see him nibble at the baited hook.

Never the sort to turn down a handout or a solid side hustle.

He asked if Becky Rant could ask around. If she could find out more about the house. She said she thought she could, maybe some people she could call on, but she needed some time. Not a ton, but the people who'd know, who she'd get the information from, were out of pocket. All lies mixed with crap, of course, but it was good enough to keep Ronald from killing her, and it gave her the cushion she needed to get things done. Her acting was so spot-on she almost believed it herself.

I would like to thank the Academy and my parents.

Whoever they are.

Later she told Ronald she found out something big and wanted to meet for dinner at their favorite place in Venice. A place off the water. Close to a stretch of beach. It was a weeknight and the beach would not be in its normal chaotic state, though it would still be busy enough to accomplish what Becky needed to happen.

It would be as close to perfect as she could get.

At the restaurant, Ronald arrives ten minutes late, as he does.

Becky Rant expected as much and planned accordingly. She's drinking water this evening. A rare choice for her, but a necessity.

"You want some wine?" Ronald asks, looking at her glass of water. "We at a church thing?"

As he begins to flag down a waiter, Becky Rant sees no reason to waste time.

"This ends with killing me, doesn't it?" She sips her water. "Dinner then an assassination, right?"

He waves off the waiter. "What the hell are you talking about?"

"You had Isabel killed. So, I'm next. Right?"

Ronald can see the half-crazed look in her eyes and realizes this isn't going to end well. For one of them. He resets, then smiles wide.

"Not sure what you think you know, kid. That pill regimen has your brains all whipped up into pancake batter."

"Yeah, probably. Still doesn't change the facts." She leans in. A vein running down her forehead plumps up. "You killed her, you son of a bitch," she barks.

"Stop." Ronald slams the table with his palm. Everything jumps, including Becky Rant. His expression never changes, a cold smile still on his face. "Lower your goddamn voice."

Becky Rant leans back.

Ronald straightens his tie.

"You don't know what you're talking about, Becky. Sorry, Becky Rant. I get it. You're a little upset—"

"A little upset? Unbelievable."

"We can work this out."

"Can we? Sounds challenging at this point."

"Tell me where the house is."

"There is no house, you dumbass."

"Oh, I think there is."

"Then find it, genius," Becky Rant says as she leaves the table, tossing her napkin in his face. It's a small touch she comes up with in the moment. Thinks it plays well in the room. She rushes out the door, not giving him time to stop her, but wanting him to follow her out into the night.

He does.

Not running, but moving with extreme purpose, she reaches the beach. She kicks off her shoes, knowing they will slow her down or give her the wrong movement at the wrong moment. Even a simple unwanted shift in the sand could be catastrophic. Could cause a mistake when she can't afford one.

"Becky, come on. Let's hash this out," he calls out. He's close behind.

She moves down to the water, a spot she chose when she checked the area out last night. She's come here a few times over the last couple of days and nights. Last night was the final walkthrough.

Ronald is getting closer.

There's a line of condos stretched out behind them along the beach, a few shops and restaurants as well. A small smattering of people are walking the beach, but none are paying attention to them.

It's perfect.

"This can still work out," Ronald says. "It can work really well for both of us."

She stops. Digs her feet into the sand, turning toward him. They stand under the moonlight, the sound of the ocean waves behind them.

"How?" she asks him, getting in his face. "Explain how this going to work out."

Ronald pauses, stops himself from saying what he was going to say, then starts again. He tries to sugar-coat-smooth things over. He tosses her a smile and sweetens up his voice. Her skin begins to have a crawling sensation. She can almost feel a thin layer of slime cover her from being so close to him.

"Becky, come on. You think I'd do that to you? There have been ups and downs, sure, but that's the way with men and women. It happens. We had some times, right? Some good ones."

Becky Rant smiles, matching his.

She looks into his eyes.

"No, no we did not."

She pulls a gun from her behind her back, jamming it into the center of his chest. Easing her grip ever so slightly, she lets him grab ahold of her arm. While training with the LAPD, she learned exactly how he'd come at her arm, the tactic he'd been trained to use, and she counters it with a move that works for her. He's got her on upper body strength, but they aren't arm wrestling here. She worked out for this moment specifically. Worked her forearms, her triceps, her core to the point of complete exhaustion.

All for this moment.

She lands a punch to the side of his face. She feels the crunch of his jaw, the rip of her skin as her knuckles tear.

He tags her with a strike above her eyebrow. His ring tears at her skin as his fist slides off. Blood rolls into her eye. Ronald throws another crushing punch to her ribs.

She takes it, absorbing the crack. She thinks about throwing a kick to his knee. It would buckle him to the sand and stop the punches. But she stops herself.

She needs him to run away.

Ronald grabs again for her wrists. She slips away. He lands a punch, then a knee, to her body and legs. She grits her teeth, letting her boxing training do its thing. Remembers what Johnny taught her and Isabel years ago back at the construction site.

Learning how to take a punch is just as important as throwing one.

She breathes out, letting the pain roll out as the air leaves her lungs.

Now is the time.

Turning her hand ever so slightly, she allows him to move the gun, to alter the grip that she wants him to have. The angle she wants him to take. She wants the gun tilted. Wants it turned in on her. The barrel turns and jerks until it is pointed dead in the middle of her chest.

A switch flips in her head.

She pulls the trigger.

Twice.

The sounds are big. Booming, jarring thunder claps of gunfire. Blasts that rumble down the beach, rippling off the rolling ocean water, leaving a hanging echo in the air for what seems like forever. As the second blast rips through the night, Becky Rant throws herself backward as hard as she can, launching herself with the power in her spin-yoga thighs. Makes sure she flies backward, clearing space from him with the gun firmly in her hand.

Ronald Church is frozen, a statue in the sand.

But not for long.

He can't afford to be seen here. An Agency man can finesse his way out of being linked to the shooting of an informant in a civilian area. She knows that. Not a stretch of the imagination. But it would be another complication for Ronald in the long list of his complicated life. There would be many questions, and those questions might open up ways for people to start digging their fingers into his operations. Comb over his judgment calls in the past. Put new eyes on his future. There will be messes to clean up with local PD, and civilians will soon crowd the beach if he doesn't move soon.

Ronald runs hard, storming off in the opposite direction of the lights and shops that line the beach. This is an area he's familiar with, one he's worked in the past. He knows the street cameras are less effective in that direction. There's a blind spot where he can cross over and out into the street as if he were simply a lonely man walking on the beach. He can raise his collar, lower his chin, and keep his back to the trouble areas of the street.

Sure, they can place him at the restaurant, maybe triangulate him chasing her to the beach, but he can work that out later. Right now, he needs time. Time to think of a narrative without the clutter. Get his head right. Void out the adrenaline spike of what just happened.

Becky Rant knows all this as well.

She counted on it.

Under the cover of darkness, she watches him run away. The cold water of the ocean washes up, reaching her hair, but not far enough to touch her skull. *Tease*, she thinks. How nice it would be to feel the cold touch of the Pacific roll through her hair. She can feel the heat radiate off from her face. She imagines frying the proverbial egg on her forehead. The adrenaline had been surging high through her as well, though it's now starting to come down.

The anger is still burning. That doesn't dissipate. Ever. A big box is being checked off in her mind. A slow-motion pen strikes down then whips up with the satisfaction of completion. She lies there as still as can be with her eyes wide open. Open for the first time in a long time. She'd laugh if she thought she could get away with it.

She hears voices starting to pick up in the distance. It won't be long until the pain in the ass innocent bystanders get involved. Holding her ribs, sucking in a sharp breath, she pushes herself up. She took some solid shots. They will throb and ache much more later, she knows. The bruises will rise and the pain will slap her around hard for days. But that's not now. Now she needs to get the hell off of this beach and get gone.

Lights kick on along the beach, popping to life in the rows of windows that line the multimillion-dollar condos and beach homes. Someone will call the cops soon, if they haven't already. She needs to move. Sliding the gun behind her back, she adjusts her shirt and starts toward the same direction as Ronald. She'll need to take the similar path, needs to stay off the cameras as well.

She has her sights set on a BMW she saw before dinner parked on a dark street. It's not far from where she parked her car near the beach. She can transfer her bags, her booze, and her pretty little hammer quickly and easily. Sure, she could pick a less conspicuous car for her trip to Rough Creek, Texas, but she died only a minute or two ago. She should treat herself to a sweet ride.

She's earned it, dammit.

Seriously, how many times does a girl get to die?

PART THREE

2 DAYS AGO (LAGUNA BEACH, CALIFORNIA)

Becky Rant and Hank park about a mile away.

Didn't want to park too close on the off chance there were eyeballs on them. The walk feels good. Good to stretch their backs and legs after the haul. It was a long drive through the night, and Becky Rant can't wait to feel the joy of sleep again. Real, true sleep. She knows it might be a while. She still has a lot of work ahead of her. Deep down inside, she knows she'll never sleep like she used to. This life she's carved out for herself, this path she's headed down, is not one filled with luxurious rest and relaxation.

She's messed with the Agency.

In a huge way.

She's about to be guardian to the twins of drug lords.

Not much downtime there.

She'll do it all gladly, with a smile and wink. She made a promise. She has a debt to pay back to a friend. Becky Rant hopes she's doing the right thing. A little late to go back now, can't put the genie back in the bottle, but she does hope that she's done the right thing for those children. Ronald will trade them, kill them, or let them drop into the foster care system, where maybe they make it or maybe they don't. Becky Rant doesn't consider any of those as options.

Will I be a good mom?

The question stops Becky Rant in her tracks. She's in the middle of one of the most beautiful spots in Southern California, but she doesn't see a thing. That question, the *good mom* question, is one she hasn't even considered. In all of this, the planning, the execution of it all, she never allowed herself to think about being a parent. *Parent* is a relative term here, she knows that. Soon they will have to know the truth. At least some form of it.

What will I tell them?

What's the right way to handle any of this?

She wants to tell them the truth, but the truth is hard and mean. Maybe she'll spoon-feed it to them in small doses. Give them a little more here and there as they get older. How do you tell kids about any of this? Maybe they shouldn't know the truth. The truth will not set them free, and could get them killed. The wrong person hears who their parents are and all of this was for nothing.

Becky Rant feels her stomach turn.

She's so close to the end and she's about bust out a full-on panic attack right here in paradise. She hasn't even begun to think of things like school, soccer, dance lessons, braces, first kisses. They will have questions, like, *Where do babies come from? Is there a God? Can I have cake for breakfast?* She feels her knees get weak. The world tilts ever so slightly. Expecting parents with good jobs and better childhoods get months to prepare. She's getting hours, and she wasn't in perfect condition to begin with.

"You okay?" Hank asks, placing a hand on her shoulder.

"No," she says. "Not even close."

He smiles.

She's not kidding.

Hank points to a small oceanside bungalow nestled down in a cove. "Well, here we are."

It's a gorgeous, surprisingly quaint place tucked into a hill overlooking the Pacific. It's not gaudy, doesn't scream, "Hey, look at me and my money." It's a perfect spot. Hidden, but not. Open, but easy to miss in all the other flashes of beauty and money. Becky Rant knew it would be perfect. Isabel always had an eye for this sort of thing.

Her taste in men is up for debate.

She glances toward Hank.

Standing in the driveway of the house, his blank expression could be read in any number of ways. From a distance it might seem like nothing is going on, but from where she's standing, she can see his eyes are swimming. Can almost feel the fumbling dance staged inside of him. There's an energy coming from him that she wouldn't be able to begin to describe. They stand near one another, but a million miles away. Together, but separated by a universe. Standing in silence, they let the cool breeze from off the water surround them, wrap its normally-soothing arms around them.

Right now, it only creates a chill.

Becky Rant can't imagine what's going on inside his mind. Sadness and crushing guilt mixed into a conflicted mess of twisted emotions that he has no idea how to express, let alone resolve. She wants to reach to him. Thinks of holding his hand. Considers touching his shoulder, simply letting him know she's there. Decides better of it. She hasn't known him long, but she knows he needs space. A quiet area for him to think. Time to process. To breathe.

"You ready?" Hank asks, letting her off the hook.

She cracks a smile. Time must be up.

She thumbs toward the house. "You know how to get in?"

"I do."

Hank leads her to the back of the house into a small, gated yard. There's a well-kept garden of sorts, with flowers and plants that Becky Rant doesn't know the names of but can appreciate their look and feel. She can picture Isabel choosing each one, driving people insane with her attention to detail. There's a hammock along with a copper fire pit surrounded by comfy-looking chairs.

Hank walks along a stone-lined path leading to the back door of the house. Becky Rant sees him counting as he walks, counting the stones that run on the outside of the path. He stops, leaning down to pick up what looks like a random stone. Turning it over, he punches a code into a tiny keypad. A small hatch flips open with a click and a key drops into Hank's hand.

Inside, the house is surprisingly cozy. She's not sure what she expected, but this place has more of a home feeling to it than the place Isabel and Hector shared in San Diego. Becky Rant remembers her and Isabel mocking Hector's drug lord decorating. Isabel did her best to bring it down, but while she won a few battles, she lost the home décor war.

As her eyes take in the place, Becky Rant feels a warmth come over her. This is the house Isabel wanted. For herself. She bought it off the books shortly after Hector died and used it as a sanctuary of sorts. When Isabel would talk about changing things, about changing the business and her family's life, this is what she had in mind.

She looks over to Hank.

Isabel let him into her world.

Becky Rant's feelings are now a balled up mass of confusion. Trying to reconcile what she's done is borderline impossible. Becky Rant brought Hank to Isabel. Hank played a major role in getting her husband killed and, ultimately, he killed her. And yet here they both are in Isabel's handcrafted private sanctuary trying to pull off a plan to save her children. Save Isabel's children from the world she left for them. There's no putting this all to rest. Becky Rant knows this now. There's no way to find complete peace with any of this, but she's doing what she can. She's owning her past. Honoring her promise.

The right and wrong of it all is up to someone else to decide.

Some other asshole can hack up the morality of it.

Walking around the living room, Becky Rant soaks up the small, homey vibe to the place. She takes a moment to enjoy the large, breathtaking picture window with an amazing view of the water. There's a perfect amount of sound from the outside world that seeps through the walls. The faint sound of the water crashing on the rocks below can be heard, but not enough to where you'd need to raise your voice to be heard. A wonderful white noise machine provided by Mother Nature.

Deep, rich woods with flashes of color from well-placed rugs and pillows fill out the interior. Carefully chosen pieces of art hang on the walls. No personal photos. *Not by accident*, thinks Becky Rant. This is a place designed to escape that other world. Isabel wanted no reminders of her life outside of this house. This place, this sanctuary, was more than a little hideaway for Isabel. This was also created as an escape hatch. An "in case of emergency" oasis of sorts.

This place will help Becky Rant and Isabel's children escape.

Hank runs his fingers over a red blanket that rests on the back of a brown leather couch. The feel of it opens a hallway in his mind. Isabel and Hank shared this couch for hours. Talking. Sharing. Laughing. Some of the most human moments he's shared in his adult life. A smile spreads across his face. He doesn't even know that he's doing it.

It's as if she's there with him right now. As if she's sitting on the couch waiting for him to join her. Reaching out, he strokes the empty air, pretending her dark hair was there waiting for his touch. He stops himself from saying he's sorry.

Closing his eyes, Hank works to scrape away the memories crowding his mind. He squeezes them tighter, fighting the thoughts. The feelings. Then, as quickly as he shut his eyes, he flips them open wide. His chest heaves in and out. As if hitting reset is causing him pain. Hurting while willing the recently-opened hallway door inside his battered brain to be closed.

Hank joins Becky Rant by the living room window. They look out, watching the sun soft-kiss the waves. The flickers of light licking the water create a mesmerizing portrait. Watching the mixing blues of the Pacific Ocean, Hank stands a few inches behind her, just to her left. Barely off the edges of her periphery. He reaches out, fingers extended. His hand hovers close to her shoulder, a hair away from touching her. He beats back the want, the wanting to feel her skin on the tips of his fingers. Pulling back his hand, he lets it fall, dropping down by his side. He can't do it.

Won't allow himself.

Unable, unwilling, to connect.

"She kept a 4Runner in the garage," Hank says

without looking at her, voice cracking. "Registration, plates... they're clean."

Becky Rant nods. She knows this already, but doesn't say so. "There's more, I think." She doesn't *think*, she knows.

"There always is," Hank replies.

Moving past him, she looks around the living room, getting her bearings on the layout. Having never been here, she's working solely off the description she was given by her friend. She turns back, passing Hank again, now moving toward a wall that separates the living room from a smaller, even more intimate room used for movies and TV. She runs her aching but healing hands over the wall, feeling, hunting, searching for a spot. Something very specific.

Hank watches, puzzled.

This is new. Something about the house he wasn't let in on. It's a welcome distraction from the memories that punch and claw at him. He'd rather not review his time in this house any more than he has to. A special time to him, perhaps the best, yet one he never wanted to revisit. Some things need to stay in the past. Sometimes even the good times need to be buried and forgotten. Glancing over to the kitchen, he can still hear the two of them laughing while failing at a simple snack. The smell of the burnt bowl of popcorn fills his brain. He can still smell it. He's sure of it. He can see them curled up watching TV. Her sleeping with her head in his lap. Her peaceful smile.

The look in her eyes when he plunged the knife into her throat.

"You ready?" Becky Rant asks.

Hank shakes himself loose from his war-torn mind.

She doesn't wait for his response. Becky Rant kicks the wall with everything she has. A painting drops. Frame shatters on the tile, scattering glass in bits and tiny chunks.

Hank tilts his head while watching on.

She kicks the wall again, punching a large hole out of the sheetrock with her sledgehammer of a foot. She steps back a half step and throws another kick, a little higher than the hole she started.

She's enjoying this. Loving this.

Hank can tell. There's an unnerving smile spreading across her face.

She starts tearing, pulling away at the wall now. Waves of satisfaction rippling off what she's begun. Attacks the wall like an animal cut loose from its rope. She'd be lying if she said this wasn't therapeutic after all that's happened. Rips and tugs, flinging chunks of the wall across the room. Destroying something is its own brand of therapy.

White dust plumes. A smell fills the house. Works into her mind. Picks at her memory. It's a scent that Becky Rant recalls from construction sites when she was younger. Her first kiss was at one. Her first fight was at one. Not related events. She learned about friendship at one. She learned how to fight at the other. Thoughts of Isabel race. She thinks of Johnny. Thinks of Ronald Church.

Hank thinks of stepping in and helping with the wall demolition, but knows better. Becky Rant's face shifts through various shades of red. Guttural, primitive noises start then stop, indicating that she's working through some things. Hank takes a step back rather than forward. She kicks. She punches, increasing the damage with each passing second. The once-pristine wall located peacefully in paradise is being laid to waste.

Almost there, she thinks.

The items on her peach to-do list are all but checked off.

Her promise so close to being kept.

Ronald Church won't win.

She can hear his voice in her ears. His cutting coldness. His condescension. Sees him coaxing the pills toward her. Feels his body on hers. The matter-of-fact look on his face when he told her what she needed to do. That she needed to betray her friend. As if he was giving her directions to a gas station. She remembers all the things he's done. How he manipulated her. Terrified her. Held her down, forcing her to watch the brutal beating of Johnny. Her brother.

She kicks.

The house shakes.

"Ronald Church failed," she whispers.

She punches.

Isabel's children, the twins, they will be better.

Better than any of them.

She screams until it feels like her vocal cords could rip in two. Her arms shake from near exhaustion. Grabbing the sides of the hole she's created, she pulls back with all that she has left. Massive slabs of the wall tear back into her bloodied hands. Stumbling backward, she sucks in deep and hard. Dropping the earth-toned chunks of wall to the floor, she wipes her eyes with her forearm. She turns, looking to Hank, then back to the sum of her destruction.

"There." In between her heavy breaths she points to the wall. "Check it out."

Hank steps forward, smirks while shaking his head.

He guesses he already knew what was going to be in there.

Shrink-wrapped packages. All filled with rubber band-bound stacks of cash. Mostly twenties it looks like.

Couple filled with tens. A few more packed with hundreds. No stranger to the sight of shrink-wrapped money, Hank estimates there's somewhere north of half a million resting inside that wall. No telling how many more walls are stuffed with cash. Along with the money, in one of the packages there's a series of files. Hank can only guess what is contained in those manila files. He's guessing new identities. Passports. Driver's licenses. Birth certificates. Prepaid credit cards. Perhaps instructions, notes on how to disappear.

How to do what Hank already knows so well.

He knows that some well-trained, highly-skilled people either worked for or currently work for Hector's/Isabel's organization. Isabel would have asked them to put together an escape plan. Would have had them research and draw up a plan. Then she would alter that plan so that those people couldn't piece it all together and use it against her. Selling information to the highest bidder is the preferred practice in that business. Hector would have simply killed the people who drew up the plan, thus eliminating the problem. Hank would like to think Isabel didn't go that way. Regardless, this was all carefully put together. Not much left to chance.

This was truly her "in case of emergency" house.

"This is how we save them," Becky Rant says with

watering eyes. She looks at the money packed into the wall as if it was fine art in a gallery. "This is it."

Hank nods, fighting back the flood rising up inside of him.

Tugging a package loose from the wall, she stabs a finger into the plastic. She can't help but think the stacks of money look like cookies lined up in a package. Thousands and thousands of cookie-dollars lined up to help turn her and two children into ghosts. Apparitions drifting into the wind. This house contains the kind of money and information that can turn someone into a soft whisper of a memory uttered by only a few that eventually fade out into a lasting silence.

Lasting silence is what Becky Rant is counting on.

Sounds nice. Comforting.

In a few years, no one will care about them. Another group will take over Isabel's slice of the pie. The Agency will have another mountain to climb. Another house to burn down. Time will gloss over the wounds they've helped carve open and move on, move past, fighting to find them. The children will grow and be hard to recognize, if not impossible to spot. Becky Rant will change her appearance. Many times, perhaps. The red hair will be the first to go. Colored contact lenses to cover up the eyes that men dial into so easily. She will need to strip away everything she's used in the past to get her through this life.

Press mute on herself.

Turn up the volume on the children.

Becoming a mom was never a consideration for Becky Rant. Thinking past the days, hours or even minutes that were coming next was not something she normally did. Long-range plans were never part of her thoughts. Now everything is different. She made a promise. The second that promise left her lips she didn't think twice about it. Her mind had been made. Set in stone. There wasn't a moment where she tried to backpedal. To shake loose from her responsibility. The weight of what she promised was fully realized by her. Her purpose is to take care of those twins. To give them a shot. A chance at a life. A better chance than any of them had.

Tugging and pulling, Becky Rant removes a few stacks of cash and offers them to Hank. He looks to her then the stacks. Not believing she's even offering, he waves them off.

"Take them," she insists, pushing them into his chest. "You're going need to start over too."

"I've got money."

"Could always use more."

"No."

"Hank, don't be a hero. Take the damn money."

"No." His eyes lock. His voice cuts through her. "I don't want that money." He walks away from her, heading back toward the window.

Becky Rant realizes what he's saying. She's not alone in feeling the heaviness of what brought them here. The weight of the guilt she's dragging around has become so much a part of her that she's forgotten its source. Forgotten she shares it with someone else now. He's being crushed under it all as well. Perhaps more. She can't imagine what's going on in his mind.

She stares at the cash. Her mind unwinds as her fingers rub the cash, feeling the texture of the paper. Cash has a special feel to it. Like nothing else. That special feel is the reason so many lives have ended, so many ruined during all this. The "root of all evil" and all that. She can't undo or change any of what has happened, but she can still do something with this paper.

She cracks a smile.

"Let me buy you dinner?" she asks.

Hank turns to her with a confused look on his face.

"Think I saw a fancy Mexican place not far from here."

Hank shakes his head. *No.*

Becky Rant nods. *Yes.*

The place is a substantial step up from the place they dined at in Rough Creek.

The staff is young, tanned and gorgeous. They move with big smiles and a high-octane sense of purpose. Almost dancing over the brightly colored tile floor that's so clean you could eat off it. The bar stretches to the ceiling, packed with every tequila there is on the planet. The air is filled with the smells and sounds of sizzling fajitas, freshly made tortillas, and margaritas being whipped up on command.

Hank looks over the place, trying hard not to like it. "Doesn't mean the food's any better."

"Absolutely not," Becky Rant says, fighting a laugh.

They take a booth at the back. Hank shows Becky Rant to the seat across from him. Again, so he can have the seat that overlooks the restaurant. No one behind him. She says nothing, plays along. She wants him to be comfortable for their meal.

Perhaps their last.

She hopes it's not.

She hadn't planned this far. The to-do list ended at the house. She assumed one of them would be dead by now or she'd be gone on her way. Never did she think she'd enjoy his company. That they'd come together somewhat peacefully. She'd like him to stay. She'd like to tell him everything that she remembers about Isabel. Like to hear everything he has to say about her too. A dinner with an opportunity to talk, share, and let go of it all.

She knows that's not going to happen.

How do the two people responsible for her death heal one another?

How do you reconcile any of that?

She hopes he knows that she doesn't hold any of what happened against him. She's surprised at how true that is. At one time she did. More a way of not blaming herself. Becky Rant hopes he doesn't do the same with her. Maybe this is one of those things that just remains in the background of people's minds. Always there, but never truly discussed. Probably not healthy. A therapist would advise against this tactic, but they don't have a therapist on staff at the moment, and Hank and Becky Rant need to focus on survival, not becoming better, complete people.

Perhaps completion will come later.

That's a thought she finds comfort in.

Hank's eyes are distant. She can't read them. She hasn't been able to since they met. He's a good man, yet a complete mystery. One that's impossible to solve. Becky

Rant knows that's not an accident. She's heard about his training. She can guess what they taught him. How to wield his physical appearance as a weapon. How to use charm and humor to manipulate. She even heard stories about sexual training from high-end escorts the Agency uses from time to time. She knows just about everything he's done. All of it has more than likely changed him on a cellular level. Buried deep within the chemistry of Hank, he may not be capable of certain human connections any more. In her heart, she knows that night with Isabel broke him.

That much she can read from him.

Becky Rant thinks of the old couple at the Mexican restaurant in Rough Creek. The ones who sat on the same side of the booth, close to one another. The ones who said nothing to each other, but held hands during the entire meal. She looks across to Hank. He's lost deep in his own mind. Seated across from her, but a million miles away. The house must have opened up some boxes in his memory. She didn't think of that, of what it might do to him.

Hank's eyes dart as a glass drops and crashes to the tile over by the bar. There's a light that flashes in his eyes, but it quickly fades as he slips back deep into his conscienceless coma. A waiter steps up close the table. Becky Rant waves him off, signaling they need more time. She wants to say something, but has no idea what. Not a clue where to start with Hank.

Will he come with me?

Is that insane to even consider?

Will he want to continue on and go with her to where the twins are? She doesn't want to admit it, but a part of her hopes he will. She started into this alone, the way she always has. Now she doesn't know. She's not someone who's ever needed anyone else. Never wanted to need someone else. Now? She's not so sure. Part of her is screaming out that she doesn't want to do this alone, although she will never say it even in a whisper, let alone a scream. She's well aware of her abandonment issues. She'd been told that it's common in foster children. The ever-present fear of everyone leaving you. Giving up on you. It sounded silly, the cliché of it all. The, *oh, look at the poor foster kid* bullshit. But if she's being honest, she knows it's the truth.

Becky Rant reaches out, wrapping her fingers in his. She didn't even realize she was doing it until she felt his touch pressing against her skin. Hank doesn't react. Still sits lost in the back room of his thoughts, offering nothing to her in return. No sign of life.

At least he's not pulling back.

Slow progress is better than no progress.

Squeezing tighter, she closes her eyes. So much has

happened. So much risk taken. So much pain absorbed and inflicted. She lets her mind get lost along with his, allowing the sounds of the restaurant to provide her with the white noise needed to find some peace among the chaos. The simple act of holding his hand is calming. Soothing her into a sense of security, false as it may be. She's not alone in this. She is so close to the finish line. She's almost there.

Hank squeezes her hand.

Becky Rant opens her eyes. It's the first time he's done anything like that. The first time he's returned any sort of gesture. One of the few times he's accepted anything at all in the way of affection. The first time he's engaged without withdrawing. He's looking right at her, tears filling his eyes, forming in the edges, seconds from dropping down his face. He swallows, fighting so hard to hold it all back. His red, watery eyes hold hers.

"I'm sorry," he says with a crack in his voice.

Becky Rant feels like breaking down at the table. Letting the flood roll out from her and say all the things she's wanted to say about Isabel and what they've done. But she knows that's not the way to go. Not with Hank.

"So am I," she says, barely above a whisper.

Hank looks to the ceiling, shaking his head. A visible war is going on inside his mind. One with no easy wins. No clear victory possible.

"Hank," she says. "You can talk to me, you know? If you want."

As if her hand were on fire, he releases it, shaking his fingers free. Hank exits the booth without looking back, letting his napkin drop to the tile. She watches him move quickly to the bathroom. A spike of anger fires off inside her. Anger toward herself, knowing she shouldn't have pushed. She should have left a quiet moment alone.

The waiter returns.

"Two shots of Patron and two Dos Equis," she says. "No idea what he's having."

As the waiter leaves, she lets the feelings of what just happened with Hank shift then fade. She can't dwell. No time. She's become a master of compartmentalizing hurt and unpacking it later. Her thoughts move to terrifying questions.

What's next?

What do I do now?

Hank shoves the door open, stepping into the bathroom.

His eyes are empty, his face a blank slate. His body slumps like an elderly man as his fingers fumble for a hold along the tiled walls. Mind scrambled with images folding over on top of memories. Smashing irrational thoughts all piling up high like a synaptic car wreck. Restaurant patrons move around him as if he was merely an obstacle. Something to avoid on their way in and out of the restroom.

Hank stands at the bathroom sink, bracing himself with his hands spread apart, planted on the counter. His head down as if hoping this will pass, even if he knows damn well it will not. Turning the knob, he lets the water run, watching it stream, but does nothing with it. His vision blurs as he focuses on the sound. Hoping the simple, basic sound of running water will deliver him from his head. Provide a distraction from his thoughts.

He thinks of Isabel.

Her face.

Her laugh.

Of her slipping off to the hotel room bathroom that night in San Diego. She was singing at one point. Then it stopped. She came out with a gun in her hand. In-between she got a call from someone. Could have been a million different people. Hank sets his phone on the counter while a child bumps into him on his way to dry his tiny hands.

"Excuse me," the little boy says.

Hank doesn't even notice the contact.

Who called her that night?

It doesn't matter, he tells himself, but the question

sticks in Hank's mind for some reason. Picking away at him like healing scab on his brain.

Was it a business associate?

Her security?

A friend, perhaps?

Hank glances towards the door as the child clumsily pushes through, letting the door swing open wide. As it hangs open, for just a moment, Hank sees Becky Rant sitting alone at their table. She's staring blankly at her drinks. Her thoughts are churning as well, it's plain to see. He can't imagine what she's thinking. The past. The road ahead of her. All that she's been through. She could use help. Help she'll never ask for. He thinks of what she's trying to do for her friend. For her friend's children. He knows that she's worried. Worried that she's not ready and, if he's being honest, he has doubts as well.

He envisions Becky Rant calling her childhood friend Isabel.

Isabel's phone buzzing on the counter that night in San Diego.

Isabel answering the call in the hotel suite bathroom. The call warning her that night that she's in danger. Telling her about Hank. He imagines the look on Isabel's face as she heard the news. The fear. Perhaps it was something that she already knew. Was there shock?

Relief from the confirmation? Hate? Did she die hating him?

Hank closes his fists tight.

It would make sense. Becky Rant knew about him because of her relationship with Ronald Church. This is why Isabel came out armed. Because of the call she never wanted to receive.

Hank glances to his phone on the counter.

He can see that call, that moment with Isabel as clear and real as anything.

The water pours down from the faucet, starting to pool in the sink.

In his mind he sees Isabel coming out from the bathroom with the gun held in her hand. The look in her eyes. He's tried to read those eyes over and over again in his memories. In his nightmares. He can see it just like it was yesterday.

She hated me in those final moments.

Maybe it would have ended differently if she didn't have the gun in her hand. Maybe they could have talked. Perhaps he would have lost his will to do the job, have been rendered useless by his feelings for her. By the look in her eyes. He wouldn't have been able to do it. If she hadn't have taken that call and if she'd stepped out unarmed, maybe life would be different right now.

Better right now. For everybody. He glances back out the door towards Becky Rant.

The door closes. He looks to his phone on the counter.

Hank closes his eyes tight.

He sees Isabel bleeding out from her throat. Blood pooling on the floor.

Just like it was yesterday.

Becky Rant wasn't sure she'd even get to this point.

Her mind turns over and over while sitting at the table waiting for Hank.

She did have a plan, it just didn't go past getting to the house. The details start to crowd out thoughts of Hank. She'll have to unload the cash from the walls. Isabel told her there were three walls in total to unload, and to make sure she remembers to review the envelopes, then alter the steps as needed.

There's enough information and money there to change the identities of Becky Rant and the twins. A few times, if needed. She might need to launder their back-story more than once. The 4Runner has clean plates and the registration matches the name on one of the driver's licenses, just in case she gets pulled over. There's enough cash to get her through a considerable amount of time, but they can't run a cash-only life too long without seeming strange. Not in today's world.

She'll need to visit the guy at the bank Isabel recommended.

The one outside of San Bernardino who will take all that wall-cash and turn it into something Becky Rant can move around to different legitimate accounts. Freely. As in, use money like a normal person playing life straight. The Bank Boy, as they call him, is so damn deep into debt that he wouldn't dream of turning on Becky Rant. Besides, she'll flip whatever work he does over so many times through various other accounts that neither he nor the Agency will have a clue whose money it is, let alone figure out and track down the missing Becky Rant and her adopted drug lord twins.

She imagines an Old West wanted poster hanging in the federal offices. Grainy black and white photos of her and the twins. They're wearing cowboy hats and solemn, hard looks.

That would be cool as hell, she thinks.

Her drinks arrive.

She glances back toward the restrooms. Hank hasn't come out.

She has no idea how to handle the Hank situation. He's hurting inside. He's broken, yet beautiful and brutal all at the same time. She throws back one shot then follows it with a slug of cold beer. It feels incredible. Cleansing. A liquid reset of the heart and mind. She can't help but think this might be the last bit of boozing she'll do for a long time. She has to have a clear head moving forward. Life with children will change her habits forever.

What will my life become?

Becky Rant, or whatever her name will be, single mother of two.

The second shot of tequila goes down.

Will I meet someone?

Falling in love with someone seems like a ridiculous idea right now. Something dirty. Impossible and unnecessary. Not to mention, her faith in humanity is more than a little strained at the moment. Looking to the restrooms, she thinks of Hank. The trained killer. The Lady-Killer. She's seen flashes of kindness, glimpses of the emotional battle waging war inside of him. A monster created by the Agency. Possibly a kind man manipulated, erased, used and pushed to the brink of breakdown. Now, what's left is set adrift for the rest of his time on this earth.

She throws back the rest of her Dos Equis.

Hank steps out from the restroom. He cuts hard to the right without even so much as a glance in her direction, walking past their table toward the front door.

"Hank," she says.

He continues moving, weaving between a waitress, then a busboy.

Becky Rant gets up from the booth and goes after him. She wants a chance to say something before he goes. Before he disappears. A chance to say something, anything to him. She has no idea if she will ever see him again. No way she can let him leave her life without some kind of a conversation.

So much to say.

No way to say it all.

The cool ocean air rolls over her face as she steps out into the small parking lot. She looks in every direction. It's dark, but the lights from the restaurant and glow of the moon give her enough to see him up ahead. Hank turns, heading toward the water. There's a small wooden walkway that leads down onto the beach. He steps down the path, dropping out of sight.

"Hank," she calls out while chasing him.

He keeps moving without a moment of pause, each step bringing him in and out of her sight line. Her feet pound the wooden planks of the walkway. She knows this is what he does. He moves on and rebuilds, letting the past do its damage.

"Hank—"

A thick hand covers her mouth.

Two more strong hands grab her shoulders.

A pinprick stabs into her neck.

She feels her tongue grow thick as she tries to say his name one more time. A strange, yet calming, sensation overcomes her almost immediately. Like her brain has slipped into a warm, milky bath. Her legs feel like wet towels slumping to the sand. Her knees seemingly disappear, dissolving into the ocean air.

The fearful exhilaration of falling down.

The untethered drop.

Dropping deep into nothing.

NOW

"So," Robot Woman asks, "did he leave you?"

Becky Rant pauses, leans back in the chair away from the black box speaker. A soulless box asking a question she doesn't want to hear. Its electric eye stares back at her, waiting for a reply.

"He did, didn't he?" the robotic voice asks again.

The room goes so quiet it buzzes.

It's the first time since Becky Rant woke up in this stark, lifeless room that she's thought about it that way. A context she didn't consider, perhaps out of self-defense. She's been so jumbled by the surges of anxiety, jarred by the sudden spikes of anger that have been so heartlessly provided for her here. Fuzzy from whatever they jammed in her neck. So twisted in knots by her situation that she hasn't had time to process what happened at the end.

What happened with Hank.

Until Robot Woman just said it, the idea hadn't registered with Becky Rant.

The idea that Hank left her behind.

Another idea stabs at her brain.

A darker, more unsettling idea.

"You know what else?" Robot Woman says.

"No," Becky Rant lets slip out as the realization washes over her. She doesn't want to hear what's next, even though her mind is way ahead of Robot Woman.

"You know it's true, don't you?" Robot Woman presses.

"Stop."

All the fight that she keeps at the ready, layered on the tips of her fingers, it all leaves her in a snap. As if a match has been snuffed out. All the life drains from her. Her shoulders drop. Her expression slumps, as if her face were sliding away, escaping from her skull. She spreads her fingers out on the table, hoping to hold onto something. Pressing her fingers harder and harder to the cool steel, she struggles to find stability to the world, something that she can depend on.

"It's difficult to think about, right?" Robot Woman continues. "Understandable. But come on."

Becky Rant hears something clank to her right. Sounds like the metallic rattle of a door being unlocked. A door right next to the dark mirror that holds her broken-faced reflection.

The door opens.

He steps out.

"You know he called us, right?" Ronald Church asks. "You understand Hank Kane called us in on you."

Everything inside of her melts away.

Her lip quivers.

This is something she's never allowed to happen in the past. She would never let anyone see her afraid. Never allow another person to witness her hurt. She can't control what's happening to her now. Her walls are crumbling in chunks, tumbling down to the ground. Her defenses are turning to dust. An overwhelming feeling of helplessness spreads over her. The understanding that you've lost the fight, knowing there are no more moves left to make. It carves into you like the sharpest blade there is.

Becky Rant blinks. Tries to find some form of moisture in her mouth. There's a burning in the pit of her stomach that she can't describe. She looks at herself in the dark mirror, sees the reflection of someone she does not recognize.

She thinks of the woman behind it. The Robot

Woman she's been speaking with.

"Where is she?" she asks him.

"Who?"

"The person I was talking to. What did you do to her?"

"Oh, her."

Ronald holds her eyes in an extended silent stare. Milking the moment, as he does. He clucks his tongue then snickers ever so slightly while pulling out a small device from his pocket. He holds it to his mouth, flips a switch with his thumb, and speaks into the device. He bounces his eyebrows with a flicker of fun.

"She's fine," The Robot Woman' voice sounds off through the device. "Thought you'd be more comfortable talking to her rather than me."

Becky Rant closes her eyes.

"You didn't give it all to me, but you did help fill in the gaps of what I did already know." Ronald lowers the voice modifier from his mouth, allowing his normal speaking voice to return. "So for that, I thank you. Truly do. But I do need more."

Ronald steps closer to her, placing a finger under her chin and raising her face up toward his. Her insides churn from his touch. She fights, whipping her head away from his hand.

"Look at me," he says with the sweetness of a

whisper close to her ear.

She opens her eyes, her stare digging into him.

"Where are the children, Rebecca?"

Something inside Becky Rant unhinges.

She can almost hear the snap coming from inside of her.

She hates that name. He knows that she hates the name and what it means to her. She thinks of Johnny, of how Ronald used his given name as a way of degrading him while he was beaten. Before he had him killed.

Exploding up from the chair as if fired from a gun, she launches herself toward him. Ronald jumps back. A pit bull has woken up, but luckily for him held back by the confines of its leash. Her face burns red, veins popping along her neck. Only the chain bolted to the chair holds her back.

He's only a few inches away.

Spit flies from her lips as she screams. She throws violent jabs and kicks with all she has left. Her eyes pop wide, a primal rage stampeding through her. She ignores the chain cutting into her ankle. Blood begins to trickle, then roll down the chain onto the floor. She'd gladly lose the leg if it would buy her a few inches of freedom. She'd give anything for this chain to snap. Anything for a chance, an opportunity to remove the life from this man.

Ronald easily swats her punches and kicks away.

She's weak from the drugs, her normal expression of violence not as effective as it usually is. She's diluted. Muted. She's been beaten down by the days leading up to this. She knows it. Her body shakes with the anger she can't release. The object of her rage, of her pain, is standing there, and she's powerless to do anything about it.

He begins to laugh, never losing eye contact with her.

All she can do is stand there in the middle of this stark room and be laughed at like a school child being bullied. Stand, shake and bleed. Her mind goes into overdrive as her body shifts into a shutdown mode. Her brain rifles through the memories of what brought her here. What drove her to be in this room right now. Mistakes made. So many missteps. Things she'd do better if she could.

She made a promise.

Ronald lets his laughter go on, increasing the volume, the intensity of it. Letting it roll. Making a point. Driving home the fact that he's in complete control of her and what's left of her life. Extinguishing any question of who's running the show.

"Wait. Sorry." He puts up a hand, as if trying to regain composure after an amazing joke being told. "The children, where are they again?"

She shakes her head ever so slightly. *No.*

"You're in a room where even the light won't find you if I don't want it to."

She looks away.

Anywhere but at him.

"You are chained up in an Agency safehouse. You get that, right? This is where we bring people and *suggest* that they talk with us. Make them hurt until they help. This place isn't on any map. It's a damn hole in the universe." He gets close to her ear once more. "No one will hear you scream. This room is impervious to your prayers."

Her dead eyes slip over to him. She knows what he's talking about. She's heard the stories of what goes on in places like this.

"It's just you, me, and my four friends with guns scattered around the building to make sure our time together doesn't get interrupted."

She swallows hard, trying not to think about what's going to happen to her.

They will take their time with her.

They will use the coming days to work her over physically and mentally. Ronald knows a lot about her. He's built an interrogation profile on her, there's no doubt in her mind. They will try to break her physically first. The long periods of pain will lead to a mental meltdown she may not be able to control. These practices at the hands of experts can remove the person from the body, your very soul lifted out in front of your eyes and beaten with a pipe.

"Again. Where are the twins?"

She shakes her head. *No.*

"You're all alone in the world, Rebecca. Your boy? Hank? He took a deal. Traded your sweet butt all the way up to me."

Becky Rant's eyes fire toward him.

"That's right. Said something about handing over some newfound money, lots of it, and leaving the country in return for giving you up. He's a pro. Always was. Nice looking guy though. Right?"

A cold spike fires through her body. She was wrong. She thought there was nothing left inside of her to hurt. No part of her that wasn't covered with scar tissue. Nothing that hadn't scabbed over. She was wrong. She and Isabel trusted the same man, and they will both die because of him.

How could I be so stupid?

She thinks of her childhood in California. Thinks of her friends, of her promise. The most important promise you could ever make to someone—protecting their children. A promise she is going to break. She hopes Isabel will forgive her.

She tried.

It wasn't enough.

"The cool, tough trio from the foster care system? They're all done. Your buddies, Isabel and... what's his name?" He snaps his fingers, as if he had total recall. "Johnny. Sorry, Jonathan. Those two are dead as hell. And you? You're getting there. Headed there. Doesn't have to be that way, however. You can still make it, kid. You can still walk out of this room."

She knows he's lying.

She will never take another breath outside this room.

"We can still come to an agreement. Don't have to have a downer ending. You can still get out of this mess."

She puts up her hand, asking for a moment. Wanting a second to think.

Ronald stops shifting his weight. He senses she's starting to become unraveled. That the seams to her strength are coming undone. He glances to the dark mirror, knowing that others are watching. Becky Rant tracks his eyes. She looks that way as well.

She extends a middle finger for everyone to see.

Ronald smiles.

Becky Rant smiles.

"We should probably get started," she says with a cough.

"I give them the high sign? That's it. They're coming

in. They are coming in here and they're going to bring the cart. You know the cart?"

"I do."

"It ain't gonna be room service, gorgeous."

She shrugs.

Ronald nods, with a look in his eyes that might be mistaken as humanity.

Becky Rant holds her breath as if all the air had been removed from the room.

He points to the dark mirror, then snaps his fingers twice.

She thinks of the children one last time.

The twins. The boy and the girl.

"I'm sorry," she says, barely above a whisper.

A gunshot rings out.

An echo rolls from somewhere close by, but hard to tell where. Voices boom, bark-calling out from beyond the walls. Footsteps pound above them, as well as the sound of rushing steps outside the door. Ronald presses his earpiece, listening to what's going on outside the room. It's all over his face. Deep in his eyes.

Something is wrong.

Another gunshot.

She hears a body drop above them.

Her mind clicks. There's only one person it could be.

She stands up straight. Her shoulders drop. A surge of energy rockets through her.

Ronald begins to pace, pressing harder to his ear.

The screams and barking voices outside the room grow louder.

She can see his plan even while trapped inside this room. He went into the restroom at the place in Laguna knowing the only way this would end, truly end, was if certain people were removed. The only way Becky Rant and the children would have an honest chance at a life was if the Agency was removed from the equation. He knew Ronald would keep this off the books. Otherwise, no way he'd be allowed this room, these tactics to be used to capture children. No one would approve that. No. The knowledge of bringing her here ends with Ronald Church and the tight group that report to him directly.

A crash behind the dark mirror.

Guttural sounds of a brutal fight raging beyond their reflections.

He knew that he needed to draw Ronald and his people out. He needed them to come out from the shadows. He knew that he was the only one who could do that. He would let them take her, then follow them when they did.

Becky Rant clears her throat. "Hey, Ronald? How

many friends did you say you had? Four was it?"

Ronald's eyes dance. Involuntarily, he reaches for a gun he knows he doesn't have. He left it behind the glass. Didn't want it to interfere. Didn't want to risk her taking it from him.

"Let me see," she says. "I count two friends down. Two to go?"

The dark mirror cracks, something from the other side slamming hard into the glass. Bits of the dark shards bounce off the floor. The dark mirror spiderwebs, cutting up their reflection into a thousand fractions of images.

She holds up three fingers while silently mouthing the number at the same time.

The door flies open.

The Man in the Dark Suit is shoved hard in through the doorway, stumbling into the room. Held up by something stronger. Someone stronger. Hank holds a gun tight to the back of his head. Ronald raises his hands, taking two steps back. His eyes beg. He tries to say something.

Hank pulls the trigger.

The Dark Suit's legs fold, withering from underneath him. His body wilts, flops down to the floor as his brains cling to the wall. Becky Rant looks away, but not for long. She forces herself to see. She wants to watch Ronald shake. Wants to feel his fear. A faint spray of crimson from the Man in the Dark Suit's blood, from his attack dog, is peppered across Ronald's face.

Hank tosses her a set of keys.

She looks at them in her palm as they land. They are to the 4Runner from the Laguna house.

Hank fires a single shot, blasting the chain loose from the chair.

Ronald twitches, about to make a move. Hank turns the gun on him. Ronald stops, an instant statue.

"Hank—" Ronald spits out.

"Don't." Hank's hand is as steady as his voice. Eyes are cold. Removed.

Ronald stands down.

Hank and Becky Rant look to one another for a second, no more.

So much to say, no way to say it all.

Hank tosses her hammer to her.

Becky Rant snatches it from the air, gripping the rubber of the handle tight. Her knuckles pop. She lets it sway, gets reacquainted with the weight of it, the feel of it in her hand. Nothing has ever felt better.

Hank steps toward the door. A split-second before leaving her alone to deal with Ronald Church, he turns, saying a single sentence that means more to her than anything that's ever been said.

"You're going to be a great mom."

KEEP UP WITH MIKE ON BOOKBUB

Be the first to know when Mike McCrary's next book is available!

You can now follow Mike on BookBub to receive new release alerts. Just tap or click below and then tap or click Follow. BOOKBUB

ALSO BY MIKE MCCRARY

Stand Alone Books

Relentless

Genuinely Dangerous

The Steady Teddy Series

Steady Trouble

Steady Madness

Remo Cobb Series

Remo Went Rogue (Book 1)

Remo Went Down (Book 2)

Remo Went Wild (Book 3)

Remo Went Off (Book 4)

ABOUT THE AUTHOR

Mike has been a waiter, securities trader, dishwasher, investment manager, and an unpaid Hollywood intern. He's quit corporate America, come back, been fired, been promoted, been fired, and currently, from his home in Texas, he writes stories about questionable people making questionable decisions.

Keep up with Mike at...
www.mikemccrary.com
mccrarynews@mikemccrary.com

ACKNOWLEDGMENTS

I say the same thing with each book and I will continue saying it until it stops being true. You can't do a damn thing alone, so I'd like to thank the people who gave help and hope during this fun and, yet still, self-loathing little writing life of mine.

The list of those people is insanely long and keeps growing by the day. The idea of leaving someone out and listening to them bitch later is a little more than I can take on right now, but I'll point out a couple.

Thanks to the fine folks that hang out with me at Bcon. You've saved me from giving up on more than one occasion. Thanks to the editors and keepers of the faith, Elizabeth A. White and J. David Osborne. Johnny Shaw, Jammie Mason, Mathew Fitzsimmons, Eryk Pruitt and Scott Montgomery for listening to me whine and bitch during this book and others. Let's just go on to say I am very thankful to all of you who've been a part of this writer thing. I am truly grateful to those people who have helped me out and talked me off the ledge more times than I can count. This is me being honest, no bull-shit here. Hopefully you know who you are.

Also, if you're reading this right now you deserve a big-ass thank you from me as well. Even if we've never met, you've been cool and kind enough to grab a copy of my book and give it a read and that, my dear friendly readers, deserves the biggest ACKNOWLEDGE-MENT of them all.

Thanks, good people.

Published by Bad Words Inc. www.mikemccrary.com

53301811R00155

Made in the USA
Columbia, SC
13 March 2019